P9-EDM-714

The air was charged with a quivering energy

Something flickered in his eyes, a brief struggle, a flashpoint instantly burned out. Then he was kissing her, deep and hungrily. For a moment it seemed he had lost all restraint, then he eased his hold on her, sliding his hands upward and burying them in her hair, cradling her head. His kiss now was full of a deep sensuality, and she found her emotions reeling. She was lost—hopelessly, totally lost....

KAREN VAN DER ZEE grew up in Holland and as a child wanted to do two things: write books and travel. She's been very lucky. Her American husband's work as a development economist has taken them to many exotic locations. They were married in Kenya, had their first daughter in Ghana and their second in the United States. The family, which now includes a son, currently lives in Virginia.

Books by Karen van der Zee

HARLEQUIN PRESENTS

982—FANCY FREE
1126—SHADOWS OF BALI
1158—HOT PURSUIT
1222—BRAZILIAN FIRE
1350—JAVA NIGHTS
1422—KEPT WOMAN
1486—THE IMPERFECT BRIDE
1630—SOMETHING IN RETURN

HARLEQUIN ROMANCE

2334—SWEET NOT ALWAYS
2406—LOVE BEYOND REASON
2652—SOUL TIES

Don't miss any of our special offers. Write to us at the following address for information on our newest releases.

Harlequin Reader Service
U.S.: 3010 Walden Ave., P.O. Box 1325, Buffalo, NY 14269
Canadian: P.O. Box 609, Fort Erie, Ont. L2A 5X3

KAREN
VAN DER ZEE

Passionate Adventure

Harlequin Books

TORONTO • NEW YORK • LONDON
AMSTERDAM • PARIS • SYDNEY • HAMBURG
STOCKHOLM • ATHENS • TOKYO • MILAN
MADRID • WARSAW • BUDAPEST • AUCKLAND

If you purchased this book without a cover your should be aware that this book is stolen property. It was reported as "unsold and destroyed" to the publisher, and neither the author nor the publisher has received any payment for this "stripped book."

ISBN 0-373-11686-1

PASSIONATE ADVENTURE

Copyright © 1993 by Karen van der Zee.

All rights reserved. Except for use in any review, the reproduction or utilization of this work in whole or in part in any form by any electronic, mechanical or other means, now known or hereafter invented, including xerography, photocopying and recording, or in any information storage or retrieval system, is forbidden without the written permission of the publisher, Harlequin Enterprises Limited, 225 Duncan Mill Road, Don Mills, Ontario, Canada M3B 3K9.

All characters in this book have no existence outside the imagination of the author and have no relation whatsoever to anyone bearing the same name or names. They are not even distantly inspired by any individual known or unknown to the author, and all incidents are pure invention.

This edition published by arrangement with Harlequin Enterprises B. V.

® and TM are trademarks of the publisher. Trademarks indicated with ® are registered in the United States Patent and Trademark Office, the Canadian Trade Marks Office and in other countries.

Printed in U.S.A.

CHAPTER ONE

SASHA glanced around the crowded arrivals lounge, holding on tight to her bag and suitcase. Fatigue and excitement made her head feel light. She'd made it! She'd set foot on the African continent. Beyond the exit doors waited adventure. She hoped.

She could not help but notice the big man at the far end of the lounge. Amid the crowd of Africans in embroidered robes and exotic dresses in bright colors, he rather stood out. He wore khaki shorts, a short-sleeved shirt and a tired-looking bush hat on top of jet black hair. His clothes looked well-used, dusty and rumpled, and it was clear he was not a tourist who'd just fitted himself out in a safari shop in New York City.

She rather stood out herself, being tall and white and wearing a short denim skirt showing rather a lot of leg.

The man was big, broad and muscular and he looked as if he belonged in a movie—a white hunter, an adventurer, an anthropologist researching tribal wedding ceremonies. No, not a white hunter. White hunters belonged in other parts of the continent.

Even from this distance, she could tell he had a cool, arrogant look about him, as if he didn't care what anybody thought about him, as if he didn't need anybody. An island, this man. She grinned to herself and let her gaze roam the cheerful, colorful crowd, then looked back at the solitary man.

He was the only Westerner obviously waiting for someone. Could he be Ross Grant? The thought was rather exciting.

Vicky's telegram had arrived only hours before she'd left New York.

> ROSS WILL PICK YOU UP AT AIRPORT IN ACCRA STOP DO NOT TRAVEL BY YOURSELF STOP SEE YOU SOON STOP VICKY.

Ross was Ross Grant, one of two doctors who ran Obalabi hospital in the north of Ghana where Vicky, her niece, was a nursing teacher. The telegram had given no indication of what Ross might look like. He could be green and two feet tall for all Sasha knew.

He didn't look like a doctor. Not like any doctor she had ever seen. She was familiar with the cool, clean variety in white who made comforting small talk as he examined your body for defects. This man did not look as if he would sink to small talk.

So maybe he was not Ross Grant after all. Maybe he was an adventurer with a past full of dark, painful secrets he was unable to divulge to anyone. A loner destined to spend his years roaming the bush. So what was the man doing at the airport?

A thin teenage boy grabbed her suitcase. "Madam, I help you," he stated. He gave her a brilliant smile, trying to charm her. She was charmed.

Besides, help was welcome; her suitcase was heavy and getting heavier by the minute. The boy picked it up effortlessly and she followed his narrow back. Moving through the milling crowd with all the boxes and baskets and bags proved difficult, and despite the kid's wrestling techniques they merely flowed with the flow, which wasn't flowing fast.

Well, she wasn't in any hurry.

She tucked a loose strand of hair back under her hat. It was a big rimmed hat, deliciously silly with its purple rose and wonderfully old-fashioned, but when you went to Africa you needed a hat to keep the sun out of your face, and certainly when you had a complexion like hers. Bright red hair had the disadvantage of being accompanied by fair and sensitive skin.

Eventually the crowd thinned. The man did not look happy. His eyes kept searching the lounge as if he were looking for someone and was not successful. Then, for an instant, their eyes met and he pushed himself away from the wall and came striding over to her. Her pulse rate increased fractionally as she watched him approach.

"Are you waiting for someone?" he asked when he'd reached her. His eyes were a deep brown. He had roughly hewn features and was very tanned.

She gave him a bright smile. He was the great doctor, he had to be. "As a matter of fact, I am," she said. "I'm looking for Dr. Ross Grant."

Her statement was apparently not what he had expected because he looked at her as if he were seeing an apparition. Granted, her hat was a bit dramatic, but did it warrant that kind of reaction?

"You're not Vicky's aunt," he said, one dark brow cocked.

She laughed. "I thought I was." She felt a stirring of interest. Close up he was even bigger than she'd thought. His arms and legs were brown and muscled. He had taken off his bush hat, and his black hair had fallen over his forehead and looked in need of a trim. He looked rugged and strong, the total opposite of Richard, who looked squeaky clean and shiny in his designer suits and Italian shoes. She held out her hand. "I'm Sasha LeClerc."

He recovered quickly and accepted her hand in his huge brown one. "Ross Grant. Vicky asked me to pick you up."

"Yes. She sent me a telegram. Thank you, I appreciate it, of course, but I hope you didn't go to any extra trouble. I could have managed by myself."

"Oh, no trouble," he said. His voice held faint mockery and the left corner of his mouth turned down. "And I doubt you could have managed on your own. Obalabi is at the end of the world."

His tone surprised her, but she refused to let it show. "Well," she said lightly, "I'm in luck, then. I've always wanted to see what the end of the world looked like."

One dark brow rose fractionally. "And how were you intending to get there?" he asked.

She grinned. "Oh, let's see. Something revolutionary. I intended to find myself a hotel in town for the night, ask for information and travel north on public transportation tomorrow and see how far I got."

He slapped his bush hat back on his head, lifting one sardonic brow. "Such as a nice modern train with air-conditioning?"

She clamped her jaws shut at his derisive tone. No, she said silently, more like a bus with bad suspension and a chicken or two on board. He was taking her for a mollycoddled female who demanded American conveniences and American food wherever in the world she might find herself. Not that an ice cold Coke would be unwelcome at this very moment.

She took a deep breath. "Look," she said coolly, "I have no idea what your problem is, but I have the distinct impression that you're not overwhelmed with desire to transport me up north, so why don't we forget it? I wouldn't want to put you out, and I might find friendlier company on a bus." She began to march away, the teenage boy following her with her suitcase. They didn't get far. Ross caught her arm, not gently, and yanked her to a stop.

"Don't be a fool," he said. "Do you know what you're in for, traveling up north?"

"Not rape and pillage, surely. I understand Ghana is a very hospitable country. Poor, but hospitable."

He did not answer, but grabbed her suitcase out of her helper's hand and strode toward the exit. The kid was not pleased and ran after him. Sasha gave a deep sigh and followed the two of them out into the glaring sunshine and across the parking lot to a dusty, tired-looking Jeep.

"You abuse me!" the boy said to Ross, dark eyes flashing with wounded dignity. Ross fished some money out of his pocket and handed it to him. The kid's eyes popped. "Thank you, sah!" he said, obviously no longer feeling abused. He took off like a shot, in search of more business.

"Listen," Sasha said, facing Ross. "When I said I could find my own way, I meant it. I don't need your charity or your protection, and I most certainly don't need your arrogant know-it-all chauvinistic attitude, Doctor!"

He looked at her coolly. "Let's not argue, shall we? I have a Jeep, right here, going straight to where you want to be. Use your head and get in.'' He threw her suitcase unceremoniously into the back, and turned to two boys who'd apparently been guarding the vehicle.

''Any problems?''

''No tiefs, mastah,'' one of them said, grinning broadly.

The other's eyes gleamed. ''We be specialists.''

''You're little con artists,'' he said under his breath, his face breaking into a smile. Sasha watched him as he once more fished some money out of his khaki shorts and handed it over, his eyes full of good humour. The transformation of his face as he spoke to the boys was startling.

''Thank you, boys.'' He strode around to the passenger side and opened the door. ''Here you go,'' he said to her, his face no longer smiling.

Against her better judgment, Sasha climbed in. Her transatlantic flight had cost her a night's sleep and she was tired; she didn't want to argue with this bear of a man and wrestle her suitcase out of the back. He was going straight to Obalabi; it wouldn't make sense to refuse the ride.

The interior of the Jeep was like a steam bath, the plastic seat so hot that it burned her bare thighs and straight through her denim skirt. She got up again and dragged a turquoise sweater out of her hand luggage and put it on the seat, then sat down again. It had been cold in New York when she had left thirteen hours ago.

Ross turned the key in the ignition and the engine growled to life. ''You can put that bag on top of the boxes behind you, if you want it out of your way,'' he said, not looking at her.

She did as he suggested. "What are all those boxes?" she asked, for something to say.

"Medical supplies. I spent the whole damned morning wrestling them out of Customs. That's why I was down here in the first place. Vicky decided I might as well pick you up and bring you along."

"What an unfortunate coincidence," she said dryly.

He threw her a quick, dark look as he deftly maneuvered the Jeep out of the parking lot onto the main road. He said nothing.

"Do you hate women in general, or is there something about me that makes you so—er—unfriendly?" she asked.

She saw his face tighten, but his eyes remained on the road. "Listen," he said, "this is no little drive in the country. I want you to understand that. It'll take us the better part of two days to get to Obalabi. This vehicle has no air-conditioning. This is March, the hottest part of the year. You'll get hot, thirsty, dirty, sweaty and exhausted, and the last damn thing I need right now is a whining maiden aunt in tow complaining about..." He stopped himself and she laughed. She couldn't help it.

"I see what you mean," she said. "Don't be embarrassed," she added sweetly. "You're quite right. I am a maiden aunt. I'm thirty, unmarried and an aunt six times over, thanks to my oldest sister, Denise. She's the archetypal earth mother and has six children, the eldest of whom has buried herself in darkest Africa."

His face was grim, his square jaw tight. "And whom you are here to rescue," he stated tightly.

She studied his hard face for a moment. "I gather you don't like the idea," she said carefully.

"You're damn right I don't!"

"Are you in love with her?"

"No," he said, the utter amazement in his dark eyes affirming the truth of his response. "Besides, she's head over heels in love with a German agriculturalist, so if you think you're going to get her to come back with you you can forget it."

"Thank you for the information," she said politely. He had it all figured out, did he? And he was in the mood for a fight. Well, she was not going to oblige him. He could be as mad and irritated as he wanted, but he wasn't going to spoil her good time. She'd come to Africa for the adventure, among other things, and she had the full intention of enjoying her stay. She owed herself a long vacation and, now that she'd sold her business, she had time and money for travel and adventure.

Adventure, yes, and inspiration to find the answers to a question: What am I going to do with the rest of my life? Selling her business had left her without a job, which was nice for a while, but did not appeal to her for the long run.

Of course, you didn't have to go to Africa to find out what to do with your life. You could do that in Tibet, New Jersey, or on the couch in your living room, but since she had a niece living in Africa whose mother, Sasha's sister, was frantic with worry over her, it had been an omen. Sasha liked omens. She liked exotic places. Besides, she could not discount the gypsy woman who had foretold her future: "You will go on a long journey and find your destiny."

So here she was, in darkest Africa blazing in the sun, in search of her destiny. She wondered how it would present itself. She had a vague image in her head of a huge sign by the road reading: "Destiny, Exit 13, two miles." She grinned at herself.

She looked out of the window and watched the goings-on outside. By the road people were everywhere—women with colorful lengths of cloth draped around their waists, carrying loads in baskets on their heads, babies on their backs. Men in pants and shirts and ties, or in shorts and T-shirts. There was a fruit stall in the shade of a clump of coconut palms and she recognized pineapples, paw paws, oranges, tomatoes. A goat stood tethered near by.

She felt a thrill of excitement. She was here, in Africa, seeing the sights, the people, the color. She remembered the excitement of being in Mexico some years ago, traveling on local buses through tiny villages, seeing the sights, visiting the markets, talking to the curious children in her not-so-fluent Spanish.

The hot, dusty wind coming in through the window tugged at her hat and she took it off and put it in her lap.

"Where did you get that atrocious hat?" he asked. "Or is this the latest fashion?"

She gave him a wide-eyed look. "I got it in Westport, Connecticut, at La Très Chic Boutique Antique."

He frowned. "What?"

"It's French," she said helpfully. "It means the very classy antique clothing shop. Too bad you don't like this hat. Dates from the fifties. It's a piece of art, actually."

He gave her a look as if he thought she was nuts. She grinned at him. "I thought that, since I'm red-haired and fair-skinned, a hat would be in order for traveling in the tropics," she said nicely. And why not something fun with feathers and a purple silk rose? Why should everything in life be serious and proper and tidy?

She'd bought the hat, along with trunks full of old clothes from the forties and fifties, at an estate sale. That hat was a masterpiece. She'd refurbished it and embellished it and put it on her head.

La Très Chic Boutique Antique had been her own business until she had sold it to her friend Caroline last month. For a bundle. The boutique specialized in old or antique clothing that had been professionally cleaned and repaired. Wonderful things from many decades ago that artists and eccentric types went wild over. At La Très Chic Boutique Antique they could find clothes no one else had, clothes not for sale in any department store or designer shop. She'd started small, and within two years she had more business than she could handle.

She'd hired help, more help and more help. Last year she'd opened another boutique in New York City. Keeping both places stocked had been an ongoing challenge. She'd gone to Canada and even made several trips to England to find more clothing at estate sales and country auctions.

Sasha smiled at the memories, focusing once more on the scenes outside. A huge old Bedford truck approached them from the other side of the road, shuddering precariously and emitting noxious fumes. A colorful slogan painted in blue and red curlicue letters graced the space above the front windows. "LIFE IS WAR," she read. She laughed out loud. It seemed appropriate somehow, sitting here next to this silent, angry stranger.

"What's so funny?" he asked.

"That slogan on the truck. 'LIFE IS WAR.' Poor man, to have such a sad philosophy of life."

"I take it you don't agree with it."

"I agree that life is not always easy, but I have a different orientation. I like to look at life as a challenge, an experience, an . . . adventure." She smiled widely. "Life should be enjoyed, tasted, savored," she said theatrically.

"You're lucky to have that luxury," he said dryly, not looking at her.

She suppressed the urge to swat him. "And you don't? Is life war for you too?"

A goat emerged from the banana bushes by the side of the road and wandered aimlessly into the road. Ross cursed and stepped on the brakes, narrowly missing the animal, as well as an oncoming minibus, painted a cheerful blue and white. "HAPPINESS IS THE SOUL OF LIFE," said the slogan painted on the side.

"There's one that agrees with me," she said, giving him a challenging look. "Are you a pessimist?"

"Call me a realist," he answered.

She nodded. "That's what all pessimists say."

He threw her an irritated look and seemed about ready to say something in return, but thought better of it. He clamped his jaws together and remained silent.

Sasha didn't mind. She enjoyed the exotic view outside the open window. After a while he handed her a large thermos and offered her a drink of water. That small exchange over, they lapsed into silence again. He seemed very preoccupied, his brow furrowed, his eyes intent on the road, which was clogged with traffic. They were traveling tortuously slowly.

"Are we going to stop anywhere soon?" she asked a long, silent hour later.

"No. We're late already. I want to get out of Kumasi before dark. We'll be staying the night with friends of mine."

"I didn't mean to cause anybody any inconvenience," she said.

"No inconvenience. They're always happy to have visitors, and they're expecting us."

"Who are they? Ghanaians or Americans?"

"Americans. Daniella and Marc Penbrooke. She's a painter, he's an engineer. Water systems. We should be there in a couple of hours."

"I'll need to use a bathroom before then."

"You're out of luck."

She gritted her teeth. "I imagine we will not encounter a gas station with clean facilities, so how is the great outdoors here?"

He gave her a quick, sideways glance. "Cleaner than the public washrooms." He began to slow down, stopping by the side of the road, which was overgrown with bushes and banana plants. She climbed out.

"What about snakes?"

"Don't threaten them."

"Right."

Bastard, she thought as she hid behind the bushes. What the hell had she done to him? She hadn't asked Vicky to send anybody to pick her up. She was perfectly capable of finding her own way in a country where English was the national language. She was a very resourceful, creative person. Two months roaming around rural Mexico had proved that.

There was a glint of curiosity in his eyes when she climbed back into the Jeep, but he made no comment.

"How's Vicky doing?" she asked.

He gave her a quick, dark stare. "She's one hell of a nursing teacher. She's dedicated and works hard and she gets along very well with the students and the nurses."

"I wouldn't have expected anything less."

"What is the matter with her mother?" he asked after a while.

"Nothing, why?"

"Why does she want her to come home?"

Sasha shrugged. "She's worried. She's a very clucky mother. She likes her chicks close to the nest, if not in it. She was very unhappy when Vicky left. She has five sons and Vicky is her only daughter."

"Vicky is twenty-three, for Pete's sake!"

"Oh, a mere babe in arms," she said casually. Denise would probably never consider her children grown up. "You don't know my sister."

"I'm not sure I want to, either."

Anger flared up, some instinctive need to defend her loved ones. "Anyway, Vicky's mother is none of your business, and Vicky can do what she wants. That's none of your business either."

"Oh, but it is," he said with deadly calm. "I'm not going to allow you to work Vicky over until she decides to go back with you."

The hair at the back of her neck stood up. "Oh, you're not, are you?"

"No, I am not." He didn't look at her, his gaze trained on the road in front of him. The hard control of his body, the steel tone of his voice left nothing to the imagination. He looked over at her then, a swift, hard glare from dark, determined eyes. "You are not going to take Vicky back home with you. Period."

His authoritarian tone infuriated her. "Who says?" she demanded.

"I says." The two short words came out hard and fast, like bullets. "Vicky is of age and she has her own life to live, and you're not going to pressure her, do you understand?"

"Oh, I understand perfectly," she said casually. Here was a man who got his own way, a man who'd made up his mind about how he intended things to be and nobody was going to get in his way. And she had the luck to spend the next two days with him, sitting next to him in this Jeep, with no reprieve from his company. Fate was not kind.

"Good," he said.

"I'm curious," she said conversationally. "Tell me, who are you to tell me what I can and cannot do?"

"I'll tell you any damn thing I like. You make one wrong move, and I'll have you back on that plane so fast it will make your head spin."

She stared at him and laughed. She couldn't help it. It had been a long time since anyone had spoken to her in that way. It seemed unreal, like something out of a book or a movie. "My, my, are we the primitive macho male. Brute force and all. I'm impressed, Doc."

"Consider yourself warned."

"Sure," she said amicably, "if you like."

He gave her a frozen stare. "You think this is funny, do you? Well, let me assure you, it is not."

It occurred to her that it might be best not to antagonize the great white doctor any further. He might find it expedient to dump her by the side of the road and leave her and, no matter how much she might appreciate being relieved of his oppressing company, it might not be such a good idea to find herself alone in the African bush. She gazed out of the window, seeing the green hills, the jungle creeping right up to the roadside.

The man was a doctor, a healer of the weak and ailing. It made you wonder about his bedside manner. She felt sorry for his patients. She felt sorry for his wife. If he had one. She examined his hands on the steering wheel. Strong, competent hands, tanned and ringless. Good hands.

He saw her looking and met her eyes. She held his gaze.

"I was checking for rings," she said boldly. "I was wondering if there's an unlucky woman who's had the misfortune of marrying you. Are you married?"

He looked back at the road, his jaw rigid. "No."

I'm not surprised, she almost said, but contained herself.

"How long are you intending to stay?" he asked after a silence.

She shrugged. "I'll play it by ear." She had no desire to divulge her plans, which included a photo safari in Kenya and a trip back home through Europe, to him.

"Don't you have a job to go back to? Don't you work in a dress shop or something?"

A dress shop or something. She bit her lip. Good grief, where had he got that? He thought she was a saleswoman. She suppressed a smile.

"I quit," she said casually. "I'm presently happily unemployed."

"Happily? It doesn't bother you?"

She smiled sunnily. "No, not in the least." Not with all her profits in the bank. "I needed a change. I wasn't enjoying myself any more. All the fun had gone out of it."

"Having fun is important to you?" He made it sound like a cardinal sin.

"Absolutely. Without fun, where would we be? There's nothing worse than boredom and stagnation. It kills the spirit, not to speak of the soul."

"The soul is immortal, or so they say."

"Then you're better off having a happy one." She smiled brightly. "Don't you have any fun in your work?"

"I'm a doctor," he said. "I work with poor, rural people."

"Does that mean that all is serious and dismal and no fun is allowed? How awful. Maybe you should consider a change in career. Something with a bit more fun to it." She bit her tongue, trying not to laugh. She couldn't help herself. He was asking for it.

He gave her a look as if he thought she'd lost her mind.

"People do it all the time," she went on. "Changing careers, I mean. You're still young. The world is full of opportunities."

"What did they feed you on the plane?" he asked then, and, miracle of miracles, there was a sudden spark of humor in his eyes.

She grinned back at him. "The usual fine quality gourmet meals on plastic trays."

For a fleeting moment there was a softening of the atmosphere around them. She liked the gleam of amusement in his dark eyes, the smile that tugged at his mouth—a good, strong mouth, a sensuous mouth, a mouth made for kissing.

Good Lord, what was she thinking? Well, she couldn't help it. He might be Mr. Obnoxious, but he held an undeniable male appeal, an animal magnetism that drew her to him, be it kicking and screaming.

It was crazy, crazy.

After all, her mind was not impressed by this man, by his behavior and attitude toward her. She was not a teenager, easily bowled over by sex appeal alone. She needed something more from a man than mere physical attraction.

And what she wanted from this man was nothing. He could take his physical attraction and take a hike.

His gaze was back on the road.

"So, I take it you wouldn't consider changing careers. Tell me, why are you here? Why are you working in Africa?"

He shrugged. "It was a change from New Guinea."

She offered him a look of respect. "Wow! What were you doing there?"

"Same thing. Working for GHO."

"What's GHO?"

"Global Health Organization. It's a private, non-profit organization that builds hospitals and clinics all over the Third World. It was started by an eccentric old billionaire with a vision, and time and money on his hands to help make it reality."

"Sounds like an interesting person."

"Oh, he is. The man is seventy-nine years old, and retirement is a dirty word. He drives an ancient VW Beetle and wears suits that are thirty years old, his pockets full of cash money. The man is nutty as a fruitcake, but he knows what he wants."

"A man after my own heart," she said. "Why do you work for GHO?"

A glimmer of a smile. "I like the fruitcake. I like the challenge."

They'd reached Kumasi, a large, bustling town, crowded with people, roadside food stalls and traffic. The sun was setting and dusk was falling fast. She was beginning to feel hungry. She hadn't had a thing to eat since she got off the plane, but she was not about to mention it. Sooner or later the great man himself would have to be hungry, too. "Whining maiden aunt," he'd said. She bit her tongue, trying not to laugh. She wondered what Richard would say to that.

Richard always had a lot to say, about everything. When she'd decided to terminate their relationship last month, he had said many things, some of them not flattering. His ego had been severely bruised and he had retaliated by analyzing her character and behavior in the most negative possible terms. She was irresponsible, impulsive, insensitive, out of her mind.

After all, how could any woman turn down a catch like him? A young executive in a zipper empire, leaping up the proverbial ladder to zipper heaven. He was handsome, ambitious, serious, talented, owned his own condominium apartment and drove a Ferrari.

She had not found it difficult at all.

She was tired of his self-importance, his pompous arrogance. How could she possibly have been interested in this sorry excuse for a man? Richard was a cliché, a cardboard cutout. It had frightened her to think about it. He was not for her. The thought of actually being married to him was terrifying. It made her think of stagnant pools and barren deserts. She gave a small shudder. She wanted excitement, adventure, challenge. Trips to Africa. A new destiny.

She'd sold her business because, no matter how exciting it had all been the first few years, it was getting much too complicated and serious. The fun was gone, and all that was left was work, work and more work. She was not afraid of work but she had no intention of getting stuck in a rut, being moved only by inertia. There had to be more to life than working, following rules, being a good girl. Apparently, Vicky had thought so too. She'd struck out on her own. Not easy with Denise for a mother. Vicky had guts. Sasha liked that in a person.

They'd left Kumasi behind and it was pitch-dark outside now, except when they passed through a small village where kerosene lamps lit the small shops and food stalls by the road.

"We'll be there in about an hour," he said, the words not yet out of his mouth when an ominous noise sprang forth from under the hood of the Jeep.

"What the——?" He didn't finish the sentence. The Jeep began to slow down and he whipped around the steering wheel to get it off the road before the vehicle let out its last dying gasp.

Which it did moments later.

Sasha decided this was not the moment to make any comments or to point out the obvious, so she remained serenely silent. Ross found his tongue and cursed, trying to no avail to get the engine started again. It refused, making not a sound.

He opened the door, leaped out, slammed it shut again. From somewhere he found a flashlight and

Sasha watched the beam of light as he opened the hood and checked the Jeep's internal workings. It didn't take him long. He slammed the hood shut with ominous force and climbed back into his seat, his grim face promising dire calamity. She waited expectantly to hear him speak, which he didn't do for at least a full, tense minute.

"Do me a favor and don't get hysterical," he said then. "We're stuck here for the night."

CHAPTER TWO

SASHA took a deep breath. "Here, meaning in the Jeep?"

"Right. Needless to say, there's no hotel or rest room around here anywhere, and even if there were I'm not leaving my supplies here unattended."

She was dead tired. She felt grubby and sweaty and all she wanted was a shower and a bed, anywhere. And food. Not unreasonable requests after you'd traveled halfway around the world. Reasonable or not, they were obviously not to be granted. Damn the man! Maybe it wasn't his fault that the Jeep had broken down, but his arrogance was getting to her. He had intimated that she was safer with him than by herself. Mr. Macho was going to take care of her because she wasn't safe traveling by herself. If she'd been by herself, she'd be in a hotel now. She should have trusted her instincts. She had very good instincts. Depending on other people wasn't always the right thing to do. Sometimes it was clearly the wrong thing to do.

"*Whining maiden aunt*." From somewhere his voice echoed in her head. It had a sobering effect.

"Fine," she said, straightening her spine. "We'll stay here." She was tough. He didn't know how tough.

His face was expressionless, but something flickered briefly in his eyes. Surprise? "You must be tired after your trip," he said then, as if it had only occurred to him now that she'd spent the night sitting up in an aeroplane crossing the Atlantic.

"Yes, I am."

She felt his eyes on her, probing. She felt him wait. For what?

"So, say it," he said at last.

She looked straight into his eyes. "Say what?"

"That you shouldn't have come with me. That this is all my fault."

Well, he was asking for it. She crossed her arms in front of her chest. "All right, since you're asking, I will. I should have followed my instincts. My instincts are always right."

"What instincts?"

"My instincts about you. You didn't want me along and you still don't. I should have stayed in Accra and found my own way up north tomorrow. I would have been in a hotel room now, with a bed, a shower or bath, and air-conditioning. Instead, here I am in the middle of nowhere, stuck in a Jeep for the night with an insufferable example of the male of the species."

He gave a satisfied little nod. "All right, now that you've got that off your chest, let's go to the next issue. Are you hungry?"

The man was unbearably arrogant. It took all her strength not to give him another piece of her mind. She forced herself to stay calm. He wasn't going to rile her. She wouldn't give him the satisfaction.

She frowned, as if considering his question. "Am I hungry? Now that you mention it, yes," she said casually. She hadn't eaten since she got off the plane hours ago. All she'd had was the water from the thermos. She was hungry all right. Famished.

He opened the door and leaped out. "I'll go find us something to eat in the village we just passed through, and find someone to help us out in the morning. You stay with the stuff."

She had many strengths, but taking orders wasn't one of them. However, at the moment it seemed that she had little choice. She wasn't sure she liked the idea of being left behind at the side of a pitch-black jungle road in the middle of the African nowhere. Who knew what prowled around in the dark out here?

"*Whining maiden aunt.*"

She gritted her teeth, clamping down on her sudden apprehension. No, fear. Fear was a better word, but she was not going to admit to it. Surely he wouldn't leave her here if he thought she were in any real danger? Would he?

"So you want me to play guard for your precious possessions here?"

"If you want to eat, yes."

Thanks a lot, she thought. "You should thank me for being here, or you couldn't get anything to eat yourself."

"It wouldn't be the first time." He slammed the door shut. "Don't worry, you're safe enough."

"No rape and pillage?" She couldn't resist the question.

"Pillage, maybe," he said through the open window, "but no rape. More likely, people are going to want to help you out if they stop by. Just tell them you've got everything under control."

She gave a dry laugh. "Definitely."

His mouth curved. "Remember, I expect you to protect my supplies with all you've got except your life and virtue."

"Thank you for your generosity."

He turned and was gone. It was so dark now that he had disappeared in the night shadows almost instantly. It wasn't even seven yet.

She took a deep breath. There's nothing to worry about, she told herself. This is not New York City.

No, this was the deepest, blackest night she'd encountered in her life, and she was sitting in the middle of the African jungle, alone, in a Jeep that wouldn't move. The night was alive with noise, the sounds and scrabbling of nocturnal creatures stirring around in the bushes by the road, searching for food or calling for mating partners. What kind of large game roamed the jungle off the road? She saw sudden visions of big predators scavenging through the underbrush, following the scent of prey, looking for whimpering maiden aunts to have for their supper.

Oh, stop it, she said to herself. All you need now is to let your imagination sweep you up into a frenzy and you'll really get scared. What you wanted was adventure. So here, you've got it. True blue adventure you can entertain your friends with once you're back home. Give them the shivers over a glass of Chablis.

Her stomach growled inelegantly. She wondered what kind of food Ross would find. Right now, she didn't care much; she'd eat anything. Brave thought.

She wiped the hair out of her face. It felt dull and dusty. No bath tonight, but she could get out of her clothes and put on some clean ones, something easy to sleep in. Turning around, she sat on her knees and shone the flashlight in the back, locating her suitcase and bag perched on top of the cardboard boxes. She stretched, and dragged the suitcase toward her and extracted a pair of loose, flowered cotton pants and a green T-shirt. She got out of the Jeep and quickly stripped in the noisy darkness, then pulled on her fresh things. She felt better.

As she stowed her skirt and blouse in the suitcase, her hands touched the bags of cookies she'd brought for Vicky. Fig bars, her favorite. If Ross didn't manage to come up with any food, they could eat the cookies. The sweet fig filling was even semi-nutritious and loaded with calories.

She clambered back into her seat and began to brush out her hair and braid it into a single braid. Mosquitoes began to buzz around in the Jeep's interior and she wondered if Ross carried any insect repellent in the car. She searched, but found nothing. Spending the night getting chewed up by mosquitoes was not a pleasant thought, but it was too hot to roll up the windows.

She found the paperback book she'd been reading on the plane and began to read it by the flashlight. She only hoped Ross had extra batteries. She'd go stir crazy if she had to just sit here with nothing to do and nothing to look at but the pitch-black night, listening to unidentifiable noises in the undergrowth by the road. One vehicle had shuddered past in the last half hour, and it hadn't stopped. They were obviously not on a major thoroughfare.

Another fifteen minutes passed, which seemed like an eternity. Waiting was not something she did well. She was a lot better at action, doing things, organizing. She was sick of reading; the book was boring. She wished he'd come back.

Which he did, ten minutes later, accompanied by a man who greeted her with a smile and said he was sorry for their many troubles, but at first light his son would drive into Kumasi, get a fan belt and come back to repair the Jeep. In the meantime, he hoped she liked the food, for his wife herself had made it and she was famous all over the area for her delicious groundnut stew. He handed her a small enamel pan with a gaudy design of pink and red roses, which she placed on her lap. It was hot to the touch.

"Thank you," she said, and smiled at the man, who said his name was Joseph. He seemed reluctant to leave.

Ross climbed back into his seat, holding a similar enamel pan and a plastic bag which contained four bottles of lukewarm orange soda, several small bananas and peanuts in the shell.

Joseph finally departed, saying he would be back in the morning with his son, Kofi, the mechanic.

Sasha propped the flashlight up so it shone on the roof, and lifted the lid off the pan. A big mountain of white stuff that looked like raw bread dough sat in the middle of the pan, surrounded by a stewlike mixture. "What is this?" she asked.

"The white stuff is *fufu*."

"Right, and what is *fufu*?"

"Cooked plantain, cassava or yam, or a mixture. They pound the hell out of it until it has the consistency of bread dough. It's a great stomach filler, makes you feel like you've swallowed a hunk of cement. The sauce is groundnut stew, made with peanut butter and onions and tomatoes and meat and red pepper. I hope you like spicy food, otherwise you're out of luck."

She glanced at the stew. "What kind of meat?"

"Don't ask," he said, digging his hand into the ball of *fufu* and tearing off a piece.

She swallowed. It did not sound comforting. "Oh, I see. Monkey heads, snails, rats."

"Shut up, Auntie, and eat." He mopped up some of the stew with the *fufu* and put it in his mouth.

"Don't call me Auntie!" she snapped, annoyed.

"Sure. Now eat, dig in."

Literally, apparently. She watched him, hesitating. He ate without reluctance, like a man who was hungry.

"Are you supposed to use your hands?"

"Perfectly acceptable table manners, yes." He swallowed. "Don't panic. It's chicken."

She found a tissue in her shoulder bag and wiped her hands. He looked at her, amused, but said nothing. She dug in, taking a piece of the *fufu* as she'd seen him do, dipped it in the stew and ate.

She liked spicy food. This was definitely spicy. Very, very spicy. Tears flooded her eyes and she coughed as the fire spread through her mouth and throat.

He grinned, took one of the bottles of orange drink and opened it. "Here, drink this. I wanted to find a nice bottle of dry white wine, but they were out at the kiosk. This was all they had."

"Oh, shut up!" She took the bottle and drank. It wasn't cold, but it was wet and at least had a familiar taste. She put the bottle down, found another tissue and wiped at her eyes. No doubt she was smearing her mascara all over, but this wasn't the time to worry about her appearance. The most important thing now was to keep up the good work, show Doc that it took more than some exotic food and a night sleeping in the jungle to get her down.

Having recovered, she took another bite, bracing herself again for the onslaught of fiery taste. The *fufu* was chewy, and the taste of it, as well as that of the stew, was obliterated by the red pepper. She managed to down several more bites, determined not to give Ross any reason to criticize her. Besides, she was an adventurous person; she'd try anything once. This was all part of her journey to Destiny.

Ross consumed his food in no time at all, then wiped his hands and mouth with a handkerchief. "So, how's that for your first African meal?"

"Very tasty," she said, "but this is all I can eat."

"I'm surprised you ate as much as you did."

"I was hungry," she said coolly.

"And now for dessert." He broke off a banana and offered it to her, then took one for himself. "All that starch ought to see us through the night."

"Do you have any insect repellent?" she asked, having finished the banana. "I've got some somewhere at the bottom of my suitcase, but I can't get at it."

"I've got all kinds of goodies in my little survival box. Let's get organized. I suggest you find a place on top of the boxes in the back, and I'll manage in the front here. I know it's still early, but in the absence of a nightclub in the neighborhood I suggest we call it a day. Unless you'd like to play some poker?"

"Some other time, Doc." Her brain was mush.

He looked at her suspiciously. "Don't tell me you play poker."

"I'm good, too."

"Well, how about that!"

"You can never tell with those little old maiden aunts, can you? A surprise a minute." She'd spent many hours during her college years playing poker.

"Why aren't you married?" he asked out of the blue.

She slapped at a mosquito. "The opportunity presented itself a couple of times, but I decided it would be a grave mistake. I'm not good wife material."

One dark brow arched. "No? Why not?"

"I have great talents to make a man totally and completely miserable." At least that's what Richard had said. Not that she agreed with him.

He gave her a level look. "Why is that?"

"I don't like being pushed around, manipulated, patronized, taken for granted. I'm not a housekeeper, I don't cook and I don't play mama. I'm too independent, too smart, and too stubborn. Shall I go on?"

He shook his head slowly, his expression faintly amused. "No, I get the picture."

She looked straight into his dark eyes, challenging him, and there was no doubt that he indeed got the picture, as well as the message. What he would do with the information, however, was another question.

Another mosquito whined through the silence and she waved her hand to get it away from her face.

"Right," he said, "let's get organized. Repellent coming up. Are you taking malaria medicine?"

"Yes. And I had a cholera shot."

"No need for that one. There's no cholera around and they're only good for six months."

"So I wasted a shot. Can't win them all." Half sitting, half lying, Sasha dug out some things from her suitcase which she bundled up into some sort of pillow. She took out one of the packages of fig bars and tossed it on the seat.

"Cookies for breakfast tomorrow," she said. "I bought them for Vicky, but in the circumstances——"

"You did what?" he asked sharply, and she looked up in surprise.

"I brought Vicky some cookies. She loves fig bars."

"I see," he said, voice even now. "You happen to have any coffee in there?"

"I don't do miracles," she answered dryly. "Do you have enough water so I can wash my face and hands and brush my teeth?"

He did. Apart from the thermos, there was a small canteen of water in the back. It paid to be prepared when you traveled.

Getting ready for the night was quite a production, but she couldn't help seeing the humor in the situation. Humor, she knew, was a great survival tactic, and she was happy to be able to employ it. Feeling dead tired, grimy and uncomfortable, she needed all the help she could get. One thing she knew for sure: a complaint would not cross her lips, come hell or high water.

By the time she had wrestled herself through her ablutions, smeared herself with sticky, smelly bug repellent and settled down on top of the boxes, she was beginning to feel like a heroine in a slapstick movie.

She didn't have much time to contemplate this. Fatigue took over and she felt herself sink away into dark oblivion as soon as she closed her eyes.

She awoke to the sound of birds, a feast of cheerful song, and she lay curled up on top of the boxes, smiling to herself, listening for a few moments until Ross stirred as well.

"Are you awake, Auntie?" he called out. "Time to rise and shine."

Why was it that he irked her so? She shouldn't let him do that. She raised herself on her elbow and looked at him. His dark hair had fallen over his forehead and he had the beginnings of a beard, a dark shadow having crept over his jaw during the night. He looked oddly fascinating, and she felt again that annoying, incomprehensible stirring of interest. This was stupid. The man was nothing but a pain in the neck.

But he was a man. Unshaven and unkempt as he was just now, he looked utterly virile. Rough around the edges. Dangerous.

Oh, stop it, she said to herself.

"I'm awake," she said out loud.

He yawned and raked his hands through his hair. "You may have the bathroom first," he said grandly, waving expansively at the outside.

"Thank you," she said sweetly. The back door was blocked by the boxes so she scrambled back into the front seat which, in the cramped space, was not an elegant demonstration of physical agility, and she banged her head in the process.

She winced and rubbed her scalp, and he looked at her and laughed.

She glared at him. "Funny, is it?"

"Very," he said, grinning crookedly, his dark eyes trained on her face.

"You laugh at your patients, too, when they're hurting?"

"Actually, no." His face sobered into a solemn mask of sincerity. "I kiss them better." He draped his arm around her shoulders, drawing her toward him, and she jerked away from him, the feel of his unexpected touch sending her heart racing madly.

"What do you think you're doing?" she snapped.

"I thought you wanted me to kiss you better."

"In your dreams, Doc." She opened the door and jumped to the ground, hearing his laughter follow her out.

She grimaced at the jungle in general, then a laugh escaped her. Kiss her better, indeed.

Yet the thought of him kissing her had somehow implanted itself in her head, and it was most disturbing. His mouth, she had observed, was sensuous and strong and promised many delights. Hah, she thought to herself, he may have a good mouth but that doesn't mean he knows how to kiss.

But he probably did.

Oh, stop it, she said to herself for the second time that morning. Forget him. Look around you, greet the day.

The world looked a lot less threatening than it had done in the darkness. Actually, it looked rather peaceful, the luscious green of the jungle luxuriant with pale sunshine and jubilant with chirping birds.

She washed with water from the canteen, using it sparingly, but at least her face and hands were refreshed a little. She looked at herself in the outside rearview mirror for the first time.

She looked like a racoon, black circles of smeared mascara ringing her eyes. No wonder Ross had laughed when he'd looked at her earlier; it hadn't had anything to do with her banging her head. She looked like a nightmare. She got back in her seat, twisted the rearview mirror toward her and, with her cosmetics bag on her knees, tried to clean off the mascara. Ross was still outside, doing some stretching exercises, getting the kinks resulting from an uncomfortable night in the front seats out of his limbs. She watched his reflection in the mirror, feeling almost like a Peeping Tom.

He'd whipped off his shirt, and he stood bare-chested in the early morning sunshine, his tanned skin gleaming, his muscles rippling under his skin as he went through the exercises. There was something tense and impatient about him, like a restless tiger ready to spring—a raw, primal masculinity she couldn't help but be aware of... acutely aware of. She closed her eyes and sighed, trying to block out the sight of him, then twisted the mirror some more so he was no longer in view.

She was in the middle of putting on some fresh makeup when he climbed back in beside her. He pulled a clean polo shirt over his head, then sat back and watched her leisurely.

"Stop staring, Doc," she said.

"Does that make you nervous?" He gave a devilish grin, the dark beginnings of a beard not doing anything to soften the effect.

She lowered her mascara brush and gave him a stony stare. "Don't you have any manners?"

He ignored that. "Why do you bother with that stuff? You're just going to look like hell again in another hour."

"Thanks. You're such a comfort. That's just what I needed to hear. I thought we were going to visit your friends? They're not that far from here, are they?"

"No. But don't get your hopes up—we won't stay. We'll have a shower, something to eat and then we'll have to go. I can't afford to lose another day." He reached for the plastic bag. "Let's have breakfast."

They ate the bananas, peanuts and the entire bag of the fig bars, and drank the other two bottles of orange soda.

"Are there any more of these?" He flicked the empty bag that had contained the cookies, most of which he had consumed by himself, like a starved lion.

She stared at him. "You ate practically the whole bag! The other one is for Vicky. You can't have it."

"She won't mind. She doesn't eat much sweet stuff any more," he said casually. "Hand them over, Auntie."

"No! If she hasn't had much in the way of cookies, she'll appreciate them even more. Aren't you just a little greedy here?"

"Just hungry. Besides, I love fig bars."

"Well, you're out of luck. Get your own fig bars."

He shrugged and leaned back against the seat. "Ah, a kingdom for a cup of coffee." He glanced at his watch. "I hope it doesn't take these guys all day to get the damn fan belt. I probably should have done it myself."

It didn't take all day, but it did take two more hours before Joseph's ancient truck drew up in a cloud of dust, brakes squealing. Sasha had spent the time reading her novel, blocking Ross out. For a while, he'd entertained himself with a journal of tropical medicine, then he'd started walking impatiently up the road and back, hands in his pockets, full of barely contained energy.

The sun was blazing hot and even though the Jeep was mercifully sitting in the shade she felt her clothes sticking to her. It was a relief to see the decrepit truck with their rescuers in it.

Joseph jumped out, along with his son Kofi, who waved the magic fan belt in his hand.

Half an hour later they were back on the road.

By now Sasha was desperate to get out of her clothes and into a shower. She'd never felt so unclean in her life. It took another hour along the narrow road fringed with forest and hills before they reached the Penbrooke house, a modest bungalow surrounded by lush greenery and flowering bougainvillea, situated on the outskirts of a small town.

The door opened before they even got out of the Jeep and a blond woman, wearing a white cotton blouse and a traditional African cloth wrapped around her slim waist, came rushing out of the door to greet them.

"Ross! What happened to you!"

"Nothing, nothing. The Jeep broke down, that's all."

"We were worried." Daniella turned to Sasha, surprise flickering briefly in her big blue eyes. Ross introduced them and Daniella extended her hand.

"You're Vicky's *aunt*?" she asked, incredulous.

Sasha laughed. "Sorry to disappoint you."

"No, no. I just didn't think...you're not what I had expected."

"I understand you were expecting an old maid in orthopedic shoes. I'm beginning to wonder what Vicky has told you about me."

Daniella frowned. "She didn't tell me anything. Ross did. I thought he knew. Oh, well, never mind. Let's go in and have a drink. You must be thirsty."

They were ushered into the relatively cool house, the louvred windows on both sides of the large living room catching the breeze.

"Sit, sit," Daniella said. An African girl appeared in the door and Daniella asked her to bring a pitcher of iced tea, sugar and lemon.

"Where did you sleep last night?" she asked after the girl had left.

"In the Jeep," said Ross, raking his hair off his forehead. "We're pretty ripe. How's the water situation? Got any showers to spare?"

Daniella waved her hand in dismissal. "No problem. You want to shower first or have that drink?"

"The drink, please."

Sasha wasn't sure which she preferred, but was silent. Daniella looked cool and clean and fresh. Feeling grubby beyond measure, Sasha felt at a disadvantage. Her last shower had been in Connecticut, a lifetime and world away. It didn't bear thinking about. The drinks came a moment later and, having downed her iced tea as quickly as was polite, she replaced the glass on the tray on the coffee table.

Daniella showed her into a guest room, where someone had already put her suitcase and bag. It was a simple room, but bright, with colorful curtains and bedspread. The bathroom was spare but functional, and it was a sweet sight.

It was heaven to have a shower, to wash the dust out of her hair, to smell the clean scent of soap and shampoo. She pulled on a short cotton shift dress in cool greens and blues and she was brushing her hair when she heard a knock on the door. At her invitation, the door opened and Daniella came in with a glass in her hand.

"I thought you might want another drink while you're dressing."

"Yes, thank you." She took an eager gulp of the milky white drink. It was tangy and sweet.

"This is delicious. What is it?"

"Soursop juice. It's funny-looking fruit, green with bumps on it." She met Sasha's eyes in the mirror and smiled. "I love your hair. It's a gorgeous color. Very dramatic."

"Thank you."

Daniella lingered by the door. Sasha was aware of a sudden tension in the air. Daniella hadn't come just to bring her the juice. There was something on her mind. Sasha went on brushing her hair, then gathered it at the back, twisted it and secured it on top of her head to keep the warm weight of it away from her face and neck.

"I wonder if I could talk to you for a moment," said Daniella, confirming Sasha's suspicions.

Sasha braced herself. She didn't know why, except that she felt an instinctive need to do so. There was something in the air, in the very atmosphere around her that felt just slightly off-key. Something wasn't quite right, only she had no idea what. "Of course," she said lightly.

"Ross stayed overnight with us the night before last, on his way into Accra. He was . . . perturbed."

Sasha met Daniella's eyes. "So I noticed," she said. "He wasn't looking forward to dragging Vicky's maiden aunt along for the trip up north."

Hesitation flickered briefly in the blue eyes. "Well, yes, but that wasn't it exactly."

Sasha felt herself tense. "So what exactly is it, then?" She knew what was coming. Ross had been discussing her with his friends. He hadn't even met her then and was already passing judgment. Now, here she was, in the house of strangers, and she felt judged and criticized before she had even arrived at her destination. She'd been thrown into a defensive position, not even aware that there was a war on. Damn that man!

She had done nothing wrong. She had no intention of doing anything wrong, so she had no reason whatsoever to defend herself or excuse herself or whatever, and certainly not in front of this woman she'd never even met before.

"It's about Vicky," Daniella said. "I understand her mother is very worried about her and wants her to come back home."

"That's right." With five boys, Denise missed her daughter terribly, was worried about her, wanted her home. It was understandable, wasn't it? It annoyed her that she was standing here in this cool white room, discussing her sister with a stranger half a world away. There'd been many times that she'd been irritated by Denise's protective attitude toward her children, and she wasn't at all sure that Denise was right about wanting Vicky home, but she was not going to discuss her sister or her motivations with a stranger. It wasn't anybody's business. She resented being put into the position. And she knew whom to blame.

Daniella bit her lip, apparently uneasy about Sasha's lack of elaboration. "I know this is not any of my business, but . . . I care about Ross and Vicky and Jay.

It's quite a job they're doing up north, you know. I really don't want to see them hurt."

"Hurt? What are you talking about?"

"They need Vicky. She's a wonderful teacher, very competent and organized." She bit her lip. "Don't try to convince her to go back to the States with you. There's no need to. She's doing just fine, you know. I know it's pretty primitive up there, but Ross and Jay are looking after her."

Why did they think she could convince Vicky to do anything? Vicky was twenty-three years old, hardly a child. If she had enough courage to come over here, she had enough courage to stand by her convictions. She had left despite all her mother's pleas. She wouldn't come back now because of them.

Sasha bit her lip. She felt no obligation to promise anybody anything. All she felt was anger, at Ross, at the whole ridiculous situation, but she was determined to contain it and not show it.

Somehow he had turned her into the bad guy.

"I'm just here for a visit, to see how she's doing," she said noncommittally.

"She's fine, you'll see." Daniella put her hand on the doorknob. "Lunch will be ready in ten minutes. I'm sorry Marc isn't here. He won't be back from work until tonight. Ross says he wants to leave right after lunch. He knows you two are very welcome to spend the night, but he didn't want to hear of it." She smiled ruefully. "Those men are terrible. Never a moment's rest. Afraid they're not going to get the work done in their lifetime. Ross and Jay saving the sick, and Marc preventing them from getting sick by putting in water systems. A bunch of workaholics, the three of them." She shrugged. "You don't change them."

"They probably like what they're doing."

"Oh, yes! That's it, of course. Anyway, it's good to see the dedication. They're working for something that's worth doing."

Sasha put on some mascara and nodded. "I suppose that makes it easier to accept." Killing yourself for the sake of zipper profits was a little harder to justify. But she shouldn't blame Richard. She hadn't been any better herself. She put her makeup away. "I'm done, at least as done as I'm going to get for another ride in the heat and dust. I'd better let Ross have the bathroom."

After a lunch of chicken sandwiches and fresh pineapple, they were back on the road. Half an hour later she realized, too late, that her hat had stayed behind at the Penbrooke house. "Oh, damn," she muttered.

"What?"

"My hat. The servant brought it into the house. It's still there."

"That's a good, safe place for a hat like that."

"Oh, shut up," she snapped.

He grinned. She controlled herself instantly. She was not going to entertain him by losing her cool. He was sitting there waiting for it. He was going to have to wait a long, long time.

The journey was not a ride in the park. They spent hours waiting for a ferry to take them across the Black Volta River, watching truck drivers asleep in the shade underneath their trucks. They spent the night in a squalid rest house without air-conditioning. They drove the entire next day from sun up to sun down, while the lush green jungle disappeared and the land grew drier and dustier, the vegetation sparser. The humidity vanished and the air grew arid and sucked the moisture out of their skin. The villages were poorer and farther apart, circular mud huts clustered together around a central compound and surrounded by mud walls. Now and then a herd of wrinkled cattle strolled by the road.

And, like the land, the atmosphere between them grew drier too, their words sparser, and they sat for long periods of time without speaking, their energy sapped by the heat, their tempers sometimes flaring into a few terse words.

There followed another night in another rest house where all there was was a bucket of water for washing. And then finally, finally, in the middle of the afternoon there was Obalabi.

"Welcome to Obalabi," said Ross grandly.

She dragged herself out of her soporific stupor and pulled her weary limbs into a semblance of order. Thank God they were finally here. She glanced out of the window with renewed interest.

Obalabi. A small, dusty town with sandy streets and one-story buildings and small shops. "VICTORY CHEMIST," said one sign. "HOLLYWOOD BARBER," another. The streets were crowded with people, and pedlars were selling rubber thongs and plastic combs and charcoal. They drove past an open market full of rickety plywood stalls, past open-air furniture shops and garages and kiosks selling food, past small houses with corrugated iron roofs and walled compounds of red mud huts with thatched roofs.

The hospital compound lay at the far edge of town, low, whitewashed buildings connected by covered walkways. The sun glared on the white walls.

"So this is where you spend your life," she said as she surveyed the building.

"Not impressed, are you?"

"I wasn't passing judgment," she said irritably. "I was merely making a statement. Where does Vicky live? She wrote that she lived on the hospital compound."

"We all do. Our houses are on the other side."

Three bungalows huddled in the shade of a couple of large trees.

"Jay and Nora live in the first one, then Vicky's, and mine's last."

He drove up the short drive and turned off the engine, and Sasha reached to open the door, relieved beyond measure to be able to get out of the Jeep and stretch her legs. One more day and she would have grown roots into the seat.

"Hold on." He took her wrist in an iron grip and looked straight into her eyes, his gaze steely.

"Remember what I've said to you," he said, his voice low. "Vicky stays."

She stared at him, feeling a shiver of apprehension run down her spine. His face was grim and determined, and not a spark of humor lightened his eyes. He was serious, deadly serious.

Well, so was she. She had no intention of being browbeaten by anybody, least of all this overbearing, dictatorial male.

"Let go of my arm," she said quietly, and it took all her effort to keep her voice steady.

His grip relaxed and he released her wrist, his eyes never leaving her face.

"Did you hear me?" he asked softly, dangerously.

She didn't avert her gaze. "Oh, yes," she said equally softly. "I heard you."

CHAPTER THREE

WITH careful deliberation, Sasha turned her back on Ross and climbed out of the Jeep. If he thought he could intimidate her, he was making a big mistake. The front door of the house opened and out came Vicky.

Thinking of Vicky, Sasha always thought of cuddly kittens, of easy laughter, of wildflowers in pickle jars, of chocolate cake. Vicky had grown up playing ball with her five younger brothers, climbing trees, nursing lost or injured wildlife on her parents' farm.

Now, as she watched Vicky come toward her, the first thing Sasha noticed was her weight. She was thin, too thin. She'd not had chocolate cake for a long, long time. Before, she'd been on the chubby side, now she was definitely of the starving model variety.

And something else. A tight smile, wary eyes. Sasha felt her heart sink as she looked at her niece. Something wasn't right. This wasn't like Vicky. Where was the laughter, the dancing silvery eyes?

Ready to make a concerned comment, Sasha bit her tongue just in time. She hugged Vicky tight. She smelled of baby powder and she felt bony. "It's so good to see you," Sasha said.

"I'm glad you're here," Vicky returned, her voice bright, too bright.

They drew back and smiled at each other. Sasha searched Vicky's face. Framed by dark curls, it looked pale. Despite the cheerful smile, there was an unfamiliar guardedness in the gray eyes.

"How was your trip?" she asked.

"It was great," said Sasha.

"Really?"

"Yes. It was very educational. I learned a lot about stamina and endurance." She smiled sweetly at Ross who was carrying in her luggage like a true gentleman.

"Are you tired?" Vicky asked. "Of course you are, what a stupid question."

"Oh, no. I feel fine," said Sasha bravely. "Adventure is so exhilarating."

Ross was leaning against the Jeep, arms crossed in front of his chest. He was observing them, face blank.

Vicky turned to him. "I'm sure glad you finally made it. Would you like a drink?" She sounded a little hesitant, as if she was not used to offering him drinks, or was not sure that she should. She's probably totally in awe of him, thought Sasha, and bit her lip to suppress a smile.

He shook his head. "I'm just delivering the auntie. I'd better run on and see how Jay's holding out and get the stuff unloaded. Any problems?"

"None we couldn't handle. We had an emergency Caesarean last night. For the rest, just the usual." Her voice was calm and professional now.

"Good. See you later."

"Thank you for the ride," Sasha said, forcing a polite smile, determined to be civil despite his autocratic behaviour.

His eyes met hers briefly, then he nodded in silent acknowledgement, sat back down behind the wheel and drove off in the direction of the hospital.

Vicky looked at Sasha, eyebrows raised. "What's going on?"

"We didn't get along very well. He's rather the dictatorial, arrogant type, isn't he?"

Surprise flared in Vicky's eyes. "He's wonderful! He's a great doctor. He and Jay both. And Ross isn't just a doctor, you know. He's the administrator too. He's responsible for running the whole show, and he does a great job!"

Waves of loyalty billowed in the air, and Sasha had the distinct feeling that complaining about Ross would get her no satisfaction. Her feelings about the great doctor, apparently, were uniquely her own, and she might be better off keeping them to herself, at least for the moment.

"They must be special, working up here," she said soothingly. In all fairness, this was probably true. Not everyone would be able to do what they were doing. "By the way," she went on casually, "you look great. Lost some weight, didn't you?" Pretending she hadn't noticed wouldn't be natural; she might as well say it.

Vicky shrugged. "It's the heat, I think. I don't have much appetite, and there isn't a great variety of food, so I'm not tempted all the time."

It sounded reasonable enough, but Sasha had the uneasy feeling that there was a little more involved. Perhaps the great doctors didn't give her time to eat. Maybe they worked her like a dog. However, this probably wasn't the time to press for more information. She followed Vicky inside and looked around curiously.

It was a plain room with a rough wooden floor partially covered by a round mat. The furniture was simple and basic and looked handmade. An overhead fan was running at full speed, and cotton curtains of African print material stirred in the breeze. Books, music tapes, board games and magazines lay everywhere in untidy heaps and piles—on the table, the floor, on shelves along the wall. A bunch of bougainvillea the color of amethyst gloried in a glass jar on the coffee table. The sight of it was comforting.

Vicky told her to sit down. A young girl entered the room with a tray of drinks. The girl's name was Saamo. She had an open, friendly face and intelligent eyes. Having deposited the tray on the table, Saamo left the room.

"How's Mom doing?" Vicky asked, her voice a little strained, as if she'd just as soon not ask the question.

"She's fine. They're all doing fine." She elaborated on the latest escapades of Vicky's younger brothers.

Vicky's hands lay clenched in her lap—not a vision of calm repose. "I'm glad you're here," she offered. "I mean, for a visit. But I'm not going back with you, Sasha. I know that's why Mom sent you here, but I'm staying here. I might as well tell you right now." She sounded defensive, and Sasha was rather confounded by her vehemence.

"Your mother didn't 'send' me here, Vicky, for heaven's sake! Since when has she been able to make me do anything?"

Vicky sighed. "She's very good at making people do things, you know that. You have no idea how hard it was to take this job. You should have heard her!"

Sasha laughed. "I did, believe me."

"And now she got you to come here."

"She didn't get me to come here. I did it out of my own free will. Granted, it was her idea, but that was all. I owed myself a vacation, Vicky, and I thought coming to visit you would be perfect. It would give me a wonderful opportunity to see something of Africa. And if I could set your mother's mind at rest at the same time, so much the better."

"Well, I hope you can." Vicky did not sound convinced. "She's going to go into hysterics when she realizes you didn't manage to bring me back with you."

Sasha took a gulp from her iced tea. She was parched. "What do you think I was going to do? Put you on a leash and drag you into an airplane? Come on, Vicky."

"I just wish she'd accept the fact that I have my own life to live and my own decisions to make, whether she agrees with them or not. I really like it here. I feel I'm part of something important. I like Ross and Jay. They're super doctors and so dedicated."

"Well, she'll just have to accept it, won't she? You're twenty-three years old."

"She still thinks I'm ten. She writes me a letter at least every other day telling me to brush my teeth."

Sasha laughed. "No, she doesn't!"

Vicky fell in with her laughter. "Well, practically."

There was a knock on the screen door and at Vicky's invitation Ross came in, holding Sasha's paperback book which he tossed on the coffee table. "Found it in the Jeep," he stated as he glanced from one to the other, his dark eyes probing.

"Thanks," said Sasha, feeling annoyed at the way he surveyed the two of them.

"Something wrong?" Vicky asked, apparently having noticed his scrutiny.

He shook his head. "No, no. Having fun?"

He must have heard us laugh, Sasha thought. Maybe it surprised him. Maybe he had expected instant conflict—Vicky shackled and ready to be hauled off to the airport.

Vicky looked sheepish. "We were talking about my mother," she said, a note of guilt in her voice.

One dark brow quirked. "Well, I'm glad to see she's the subject of amusement. I rather had the impression she was a source of concern." He moved toward the door. "I'll see you later. Jay told me we're invited for dinner."

Vicky nodded. "Yes. See you later."

The screen door slammed behind him and Vicky jumped to her feet. "I'll show you your room."

It was spartan, like the living room. There was a narrow bed, a small table and a straight chair, some shelves and hooks for clothes. The window had a screen in front of it. It looked like a nun's cell.

"It's not the Hilton, but I hope it will do," Vicky said. "There's no air-conditioning, but at night it cools down. This is the Sahel, you know. Not far from the Sahara."

"I wasn't expecting the Hilton, Vicky. Don't worry about it. I'm here to see you, and to see Africa. A tiny part of it at any rate." She put her suitcase on the bed and opened it. "I brought you some goodies from home. Your mom went into a baking spree when she knew I was coming to see you." She dug out a tin can and handed it over. "Chocolate chip walnut cookies. And I brought you some fig bars, only Ross and I had one of the bags for breakfast the morning after we got stranded." Ross had radioed Jay from the Penbrookes' house, letting him know they'd be delayed coming back.

Vicky clutched the bounty to her chest. "Wow, great," she said cheerily. "Haven't had those forever."

Sasha looked up at Vicky. Her voice had sounded a little too casual. "Well, let's have some right now. I'd love a cup of coffee if you have one." She still felt dull and a little light-headed. Coffee might help.

"Oh, no," Vicky said hastily "I mean, we can have the coffee, but I'd rather save these for a special treat, to share with the others. Would you mind terribly? We always share, you know."

"Of course I don't mind."

"Food is hard to get," Vicky went on. "Sometimes we go to Burkina Faso and go shopping in Ouagadougou. They've got lots of wonderful stuff there, all imported from France—peaches and apples and cheese. But it's quite a trip, so it's not something we do every week." She moved to the door. "Let me put these away."

"Sure, whatever you like." She stared after Vicky as she left the room. This was not like her. The Vicky she knew would sit down with a bag of cookies and demolish half of it in one sitting. She shrugged and stared out of the window, at the cluster of circular red mud huts with their grass-thatched roofs. A pig rooted in the dry soil. A woman wrapped in a colorful cloth, a load of bananas balanced on her head, swayed by, her gait straight and elegant. This was a different world, obviously. And different environments changed people's behavior. It had to.

* * *

Later that evening she was sitting directly opposite Ross on Jay and Nora Branscom's big veranda. She sipped her gin and lime and wished he weren't there. He kept looking at her, or maybe it was her imagination. It was certainly hard not to look at him. Wearing white cotton pants and a casual open-necked shirt, he looked cool and crisp and utterly masculine.

She looked away, surveying the rest of the guests.

"We like to get together when one of us has company," Vicky had explained earlier. "We share our visitors too."

"We," Sasha discovered, were Jay and his wife Nora, Ross, Vicky and Jochen, the German agriculturalist, two Peace Corps volunteers who taught at the technical school in town, a graying female Danish anthropologist who smoked a pipe, and a skinny Irish linguist who said he was studying the local language and committing it to paper.

It was an eclectic group of people, and Sasha listened with interest to an even more eclectic conversation.

She had slept like the dead for two hours this afternoon, and, after a shower and another glass of iced tea, she'd felt quite restored. She'd pulled on a long, brightly flowered skirt, and a sleeveless silk shirt, piled her hair on top of her head and felt ready to meet "the others."

Jay and Nora Branscom's bungalow was larger than Vicky's, but simple and unassuming. Yet it had the definite feel of a home, a place where people lived comfortably and happily. The large living room sported an overhead fan that stirred the air briskly into coolness. The furniture, like Vicky's, was locally made, and one wall was completely covered by shelves full of books. The place was decorated with all kinds of African art and artefacts—woven and printed wall hangings, huge baskets, carvings, pottery. There was no TV and no VCR that Sasha could see.

"How about another drink?" Jay asked her. He was tall and lean, with a steel gray mop of hair. He was friendly and casual, as was his wife, Nora, a tiny woman with a graying, straight bob that made her look very French, which she wasn't. Nora was a nurse midwife and visited small villages helping traditional midwives improve their skills and techniques.

Sasha handed Jay her glass. "Thanks, yes."

People asked her about her trip and her first impressions about the country. She was aware of Ross's scrutiny as she talked, saying she'd found it all fascinating and enlightening, knowing he was waiting to hear her complain about the heat, the dirt, the dust, the food, about the absence of modern facilities and conveniences. If she'd wanted modern facilities and conveniences, hamburgers and steaks on the grill, she should have stayed at home where such luxuries flourished.

She tried to avoid his gaze, smiling sunnily as she talked, yet all the while she felt a strange tension. The air seemed, somehow, charged, her body tingling with the awareness of him, as if something in the air touched her physically. And the words echoed in her head. "*Remember what I told you.*" She took a swallow of her gin and lime, listening absently to the conversation, which for the moment concerned a patient in the hospital.

"*He's wonderful,*" Vicky had said. "*He's a great doctor.*" And a great administrator too, she had said.

Well, that didn't make him a great man.

So why did she feel this way in his presence? Why couldn't she keep her eyes off him?

He seemed different here than with her on the road. She couldn't immediately pinpoint what it was, until it hit her that he was relaxed now, the restlessness gone.

He hadn't liked being away from the hospital.

"So, how long will you be with us?" Jay asked her.

"Depends on how long Vicky will have me," she said lightly, aware of Ross's eyes on her. "Coming to Africa is quite an opportunity and I'm interested to get to know the place a little." *Maybe I'll find my destiny here*, she added silently, swallowing a grin. It wasn't the sort of thing you said out loud, not to mention the gypsy fortune-teller.

"Most visitors take one look at the dust and dryness of Obalabi and decide they've seen all there is to see and move on."

"Oh, but there must be more to the place than dust and drought. You've all been here for a long time," she commented, looking from one to the other. "You obviously found something worth staying for."

Ross's eyes narrowed and she widened her smile. "Don't look so suspicious, Ross," she said cheerfully.

She asked questions about the hospital, the work, the people, and Jay seemed eager enough to answer her queries, suggesting that perhaps tomorrow she should go with Ross on his rounds. "He's got some interesting cases," he said.

She felt the immediate sharpening of tension.

"She may not be all that intrigued by tropical medicine," Ross said dryly.

"Oh, but I am," she said, before she could stop herself. She grinned. "I have a very broad sphere of interests."

She felt Ross's eyes on her.

"She plays poker, too, she told me, and she likes wearing ugly hats."

"Ross!" Nora said, laughing.

"On a three-day trip you get to know each other," he said dryly. "Don't worry, she's tough as nails, aren't you, Auntie?"

She offered the gathered company a brilliant smile. "He's quite afraid of me, actually, but he hides it well."

There was general hilarity, but Vicky looked mildly shocked. Jay gave a hoot of laughter. "Well, well, Ross. You'd better watch out with this one."

Dinner consisted of rice, a simple sauce of vegetables and small pieces of beef, and fried plantain. Everyone ate heartily of the plain fare, and even more heartily of the bounty of chocolate chip walnut cookies Vicky had brought to share; they were gone in no time at all.

Sasha enjoyed the evening, the people, the conversation—a gathering very different from any she'd attended at home. There was something special about living in such an alien, isolated place, something that drew people together and made them depend on each other for everything—friendship, food, help, entertainment.

She'd watched Vicky surreptitiously all evening. She was happy and cheerful and perfectly at ease with the others. She laughed freely and spontaneously, and she was obviously very much in love with Jochen. Sasha had no trouble understanding why. Jochen was a nice guy, friendly, attentive, and enthusiastic about his work. He had warm brown eyes that kept looking at Vicky adoringly.

Denise had not mentioned Jochen. It was quite possible her daughter had not informed her of his existence. Sasha had no trouble understanding that, too. Denise would wail that if Vicky married a German agriculturalist working in Africa her daughter would be lost to her forever in one foreign country or another.

Despite Vicky's cheerfulness, Sasha could not dispel the feeling that Vicky wasn't too eager to see her. She hadn't misread the wariness in her eyes and the strange tone of her voice when she'd arrived this afternoon. She wasn't imagining Ross's watchful eyes on her all the time.

She sighed and pushed the thought away and drank her coffee.

Soon after that, people began to leave. Vicky was going home with Jochen to search through a new bounty of paperback books he'd received that day from a colleague leaving the country. Books were apparently a much-treasured commodity.

Sasha looked at Vicky. "You share books, too."

Vicky smiled. "Yeah. I'll be home in a little while." She glanced hesitantly at Ross. "Maybe Ross will walk back with you."

"Oh, that isn't necessary," she said. "If I concentrate, I think I can find the place all by myself."

Ross came to his feet. "I'm leaving anyway," he said.

They walked together in the cool darkness filled with unfamiliar sounds and smells. She was oddly aware of him, the big bulk of him so close to her, as if his body emanated a kind of energy.

"What's going on with Vicky?" she asked, wondering if she should even bother to ask. If there was something she was supposed to know, he would have told her.

He raised his brows. "What do you mean?" His face was shadowed in the faint light of the moon, giving it a somewhat mysterious look.

"She's different, I don't know. She's acting funny."

"Life here changes people." He spoke with the voice of authority. "There's no way it can't."

Well, maybe that was it.

No, it wasn't.

"Is it normal to lose so much weight?"

"It's not unusual. The heat often takes away your appetite. I'm sure you've noticed."

So she had. She had eaten little the last few days. Maybe she was imagining things. A vision sprang into her mind. Denise, in her kitchen, packing cookies in the round can. "*Maybe I shouldn't worry, but I do. I can't help it. I just have this uneasy feeling, I don't know why.*"

She hadn't paid much attention. Denise was always having feelings, intuitions, premonitions about her children. Denise could drive you nuts. And, with her only daughter being in darkest Africa full of imagined and unimagined dangers, Denise's feelings and intuitions and premonitions were running rampant, strangling her poor mother's heart like a tangle of viny weeds.

Now Sasha was having a very uneasy feeling herself.

But the good doctor had said there was no reason to worry. But then again, why should she trust him? He had an agenda of his own.

It would be nice to know what it was.

She awoke the next morning to the sounds of squawking chickens. It was still early, but Vicky had already left for the hospital. In the kitchen she found Saamo, who offered her coffee in a cracked cup and conversation in fractured English. The kitchen was a minuscule room with a small stove, a small refrigerator and a cupboard with its legs sitting in cans of water. To keep the bugs out, said Saamo. Also, there was a note from Vicky.

> Good morning. Take it easy today, but if you like you can walk up to the hospital and see our under-fives clinic in session. We start at nine. Ross starts his rounds at eight, if you want to catch him at that. Vicky.

With no shopping malls or museums in the immediate area, this was as good an offer as she was likely to get. It made her smile. Actually, it was a lot better than a shopping mall or museum. This was Africa, and seeing Vicky at work would be interesting.

After she had eaten some breakfast of plain bread with mango jam and some sliced paw paw, she showered and dressed in a short white skirt and a loose cobalt blue shirt. Then she set off for the hospital, which gleamed white and serene in the morning light.

A pretty African nurse in an immaculate white uniform showed her the way to the doctors' lounge and told her to wait while she went in search of Dr. Grant. He came breezing in only minutes later, wearing a white coat, a stethoscope dangling out of one of the pockets.

"Good morning," he said, faint surprise flitting across his clean-shaven face.

Her heart leaped in her chest. "Hi." He looked different. An unexpected rush of warmth suffused her. Was it just the white coat that did it? He looked every inch the competent medical man, imposing and trustworthy. And very attractive.

"I had not expected to see you here," he said in a very competent, professional medical-man voice.

"Why not?"

"I thought you'd be asleep till noon."

She laughed. She couldn't remember the last time she'd slept till noon. "Not me. I'm raring to go. Show me the sights, Doc."

"Come with me." He took a white lab coat off a hook and tossed it to her. "Here, put this on." He turned without preamble, and marched out of the door. Quickly putting her arms through the sleeves, she followed him through several breezeways into a ward with ten beds, all of them containing male patients.

She watched with interest as he spoke to the patients in the local language, but there was no need for her to understand the words. It was all in the sound of his voice, the smile in his eyes, the gentleness of his touch. There was nothing there now of the overbearing, impatient man with whom she had spent the last few days and nights traveling across the country in a dusty Jeep.

He was a doctor, a thoroughly professional man. He was calm and in control, the restless tiger in him subdued, or at least restrained.

He pulled up a chair and talked for ten minutes with a dignified old man with sharp eyes. Tribal scars ploughed through the man's wrinkled cheeks. He had had his right leg amputated five days earlier. He'd broken the leg, then, afraid to get western medical help, he'd ended up with gangrene. By the time his relatives had finally taken him to the hospital it had been too late to save the leg.

"Why didn't he come sooner?" she asked after they left for another ward. "It must have hurt like crazy."

"Fear. The story is that you die in the hospital, which is a self-fulfilling prophesy. If you wait too long to come, it's too late for us to help, and many people do die in the hospital, totally unnecessarily, out of ignorance. It's one of the biggest frustrations we have."

"What were you telling that old man?"

"I tried to explain that, had he come earlier, he wouldn't have lost his leg, and that if he had waited another day, he would have died. I try to explain it hoping he'll go back to the village and change people's fears." He shrugged. "We try."

They went on to the women's ward, then to the children's ward. The children's eyes lit up when they saw him. He had a smile, a touch, a hug, for each of them.

"Look at this young man," he said, helping a boy of about ten out of his bed. "He's never been able to walk normally. He had a birth defect and his feet were turned the wrong way. He had his last operation last week and now he's as good as new." He shook his head. "It should have been corrected while he was a baby."

And on it went, until it was time for the under-fives clinic. He pointed out the way, and she thanked him for the tour.

His eyes met hers for a moment, and it seemed that she saw a question lurking in the dark depths. "Don't mention it," he said then, and turned.

The clinic was a large room with long wooden benches, a blackboard, and, on the walls, cartoon-type posters extolling the virtues of breast-feeding, safe water, inoculations.

The benches were full of women draped in bright-colored clothes, with babies and young children sitting on their laps or tied on their backs. And every single one of them stared at Sasha as she entered the room.

She smiled at them, feeling uncomfortable, realizing that for the first time in her life she was in the unique position of being the only white woman in a roomful of African women and children. And a white woman with bright red hair at that. A rarity, a curiosity that obviously needed close scrutiny.

"Good morning," she said.

The women smiled or laughed, saying something she did not understand. Probably a greeting in the tribal language. The children whispered and giggled, or simply stared with wide eyes.

Suddenly all eyes left her and heads swiveled toward the door as Ross came striding in. He greeted the women, then turned to Sasha. "Have you seen Vicky yet?"

She shook her head. "I think we're all waiting for her."

"Well, I see you are making yourself useful serving as the entertainment until the real show begins," he said evenly.

She laughed, the humor of the situation getting the better of her. "I hadn't counted on being a side-show freak, but life is full of interesting experiences."

"Isn't it, though?" he said dryly, his eyes meeting hers. He moved to stand next to her, took a strand of her hair in his hand, and said something she couldn't understand to the women. Laughter erupted.

"What did you say?"

"I told them that in my country all witches have red hair."

"You didn't!"

His mouth quirked. "No, I didn't. If I had, they would have been out of here in a flash, and they wouldn't have laughed."

"Do people believe in witches?"

"It's not a subject that's discussed, but strange things happen. There's a belief in juju, witchcraft, and it's still practiced. It's not to be laughed at."

Vicky appeared in the room, accompanied by two Ghanaian nursing students, who looked at Sasha curiously.

After a brief discussion with Vicky, Ross left, and Vicky introduced her to the two student nurses who assisted with the clinic.

Sasha spent the new few hours observing the procedure, which was a combination of a nutrition lesson and an examination of the babies and children. She loved the children, their big, curious eyes, their sense of fun, but it was obvious that they seemed a little frightened of her. It was a strange experience to be considered an object of fear.

And, as she watched Vicky at work, she wondered what other strange experiences were awaiting her, and the thought filled her with a sense of excitement, and some apprehension. Definitely some apprehension.

One thing that Sasha noticed about life in Obalabi was that there was a lot of togetherness in the small expatriate community. They congregated frequently—for meals, for drinks, to swap books, to borrow things, to pass on news. Sasha loved these get-togethers. The people were interesting, the talk stimulating. They all knew each other well.

Ross, she noticed, was not often present at these gatherings. He held himself somewhat aloof and spent many nights at the hospital working in his office. Everyone, however, held Ross in high esteem. Not only was he considered a brilliant physician, but he had the hospital running like a well-oiled machine as well. This was, in everyone's opinion, a feat of major proportions in a country battling the lack of money, resources, and supplies.

Ross, Sasha learned, was divorced. His wife had been a beautiful society girl from New York who'd worried a lot about her nails. Much more Sasha did not find out. Angela was not considered an interesting topic of conversation.

Sasha wondered about Angela and why the marriage had broken up. Perhaps it had had something to do with her nails. She looked down at her own. They were very nice nails, carefully painted in honey peach.

"Joe's in town," Vicky announced one afternoon. "He's throwing a party. We're all invited."

"Who's Joe?" asked Sasha, who hadn't heard of any Joe in or out of Obalabi.

"Joe Doranga," said Vicky. Joe Doranga, Vicky explained, was the local variety of hometown boy made good. Joe Doranga was the son of a local village chief and he had made good all the way in America. At Harvard Business School, to be precise. His tribal name, too much to handle for the bright boys and girls of Harvard, had been simplified to Joe.

Joe now owned a large and thriving business in engineering and construction supplies in Accra and was involved in politics. He had a big house built in Obalabi to which he retreated on occasion to relax and recuperate from the strain and stress of his busy life in the capital.

Joe's lavish parties were awaited with much anticipation by people from far and wide, so said Vicky. "Wait till you see his house," she said.

Saturday night Jay and Nora drove the two of them to the party.

Joe Doranga's house reposed in isolated splendor on the other side of town. Sasha looked in amazement at the large, modern dwelling, which looked out of place against its backdrop of small houses and huts of the town.

"Joe's loaded," Vicky said, after they'd been greeted by the host and handed a drink. Sasha glanced over at Joe Doranga. He was tall, handsome and dressed in fashionable Western clothes, and exuded worldly sophistication. It was difficult to believe this man had grown up in a mud-hut village.

"He's not here often," Vicky went on, "but when he is, he always throws a party. Oh, there's Jochen." Vicky took off like a shot, leaving Sasha with Jay and Nora, who took her around and introduced her to some of the guests.

"Is Ross not coming?" she asked casually, having seen no sign of him.

"He's still working," Jay answered. "And he's waiting for a call from the States. He may come by later, he said."

Which he did. Sasha watched him come into the room an hour later, and her heart leaped in her chest, much to her annoyance. He moved over to the bar and got a drink, and then, seeing her standing near by, came over to her.

"All alone?" he asked.

"I'd just got myself another drink. Quite a party, this."

"You like parties?" he asked, raising one dark brow in question. There was a vaguely censorious tone to his voice and it annoyed her.

"Oh, yes," she said brightly. "Don't you?"

He took a sip from his drink. "Not particularly."

This was, of course, no great news. The man had better things to do than go to parties. He had a hospital to run and patients to take care of.

"This is quite a house to be sitting here," Sasha said, changing the subject. She surveyed the modern furniture and Western-style decoration of the room. "It's not what I expected to find here, in this part of the country."

"People often build big houses in their home villages or towns after they've made their fortunes in Accra," said Ross. Smaller houses were constructed in the back of the compound for the relatives, he explained. The relatives looked after the place while the owner was in Accra. "African socialism," he said. "You make money, you take care of everyone in your extended family." He took a sip of his drink. "He's done very well for his village—built a water-well and put in an irrigation system, which only works as long as there's water in the stream, but it's better than nothing."

She hadn't spoken to Ross for several days, although every morning she saw him leave to go to the hospital. While she sat in the living room with her first cup of coffee, which was a revolting instant brew, she would see Ross come out of his house and walk down the road toward the hospital. He never looked at the house, and he probably had no idea she watched him. She didn't do it on purpose. It was just the way it happened, yet still she knew that, perversely, she was looking forward to seeing him move past with his easy, confident stride, his black hair gleaming wet from the shower.

He looked good now, in his tan pants and short-sleeved, well-cut bush jacket, which accentuated his wide shoulders.

"Have you had enough of it yet?" he asked.

"Enough of what? The party? We just got here an hour ago."

"No, not the party. The glamorous life in Obalabi."

She smiled brightly. "Oh, no. Not in the least. I'm having a great time."

Her life was filled with new experiences and, despite the heat, she felt energized and excited.

"Oh, you are? And what do you do to entertain yourself?"

"I've been writing letters to my grandparents in the retirement home," she said piously. This, in fact, was true. "And I'm studying West African witchcraft. Juju. I've found a deliciously creepy book." This, too, was true. "And I've been shopping." She smiled sunnily. "I love the shops, especially the names. Lucky Luke Butchery, Paris Tailor. And the market. Now, the market is fascinating."

This drew a skeptical look. "Piles of guinea corn? Pots and pans? Flies? Naked children? Dirt? You find that fascinating?"

"Absolutely," she said. "It's all so colorful, and I like the market women." She wasn't going to tell him that some of it had been rather a shock. The dirt and the smells had been overwhelming at times, but a lot depended on your perspective, and she was determined to look at the positive side of things. Even more so because he seemed so convinced that she would find the place intolerable. He seemed to think that by now she would be ready to flee in horror.

Well, she wasn't going to.

She was basically a curious, open-minded person. She was going to enjoy this new experience, whether Dr. Grant wanted her to or not. And the market had definitely been a new experience, different from anything she was used to. She enjoyed bargaining, using fingers and hands and any gestures she could think of. The laughter of the women was boisterous and genuine, their friendliness real. A lot different from New York where sales people seemed to think they were doing you a favor by serving you.

"And what do you find to buy in that shoppers' paradise?"

"Market cloth," she said without hesitation. She'd bought a stack of lengths, all colors, all designs. The temptation of the exotic fabrics was simply too much. "It's all very educational," she went on. "I can even count to ten now."

"A miracle a minute," he said dryly. "But let me give you a piece of advice. Stay away from juju. You don't know what you're getting yourself into. People may not take kindly to your probings. Now, if you'll excuse me?" He took off toward the bar to find himself another drink.

All through the evening, as she talked to Joe and his guests, she was aware of Ross. He seemed to have no shortage of female attention. Joe's sister, who looked like an exotic model in her long, strapless evening gown, talked to him for a long time, and a female Peace Corps volunteer was obviously enamored of him. As was Christine the anthropologist. Sasha was not surprised. Ross was handsome, single and available. His compelling dark looks and his enigmatic expression presented a challenge. Being a female herself, she had no trouble figuring out what it was they were thinking. What passions lurked behind that cool composure? What would it take to bring them out?

She became aware of a growing annoyance as she watched Ross talking to the other women, who gazed at him with rapt attention.

Maybe it wasn't really annoyance. Maybe it was something different altogether. She didn't like the adoring way those women were looking at him. It made her feel . . . *threatened*.

You're jealous, a nasty little demon inside her whispered, and at the same time his eyes met hers. A cold wave of shock went racing through her. Then heat washed over her.

Jealous! came the ugly echo in her mind. *Jealous*! *Jealous*! *Jealous*!

CHAPTER FOUR

"IS SOMETHING wrong?"

The voice swam into her consciousness. Sasha blinked, feeling a strong arm around her, supporting her. Surfacing out of a gray fog, she managed to focus her eyes on the face looking down at her. It was Ross, his face professionally concerned, his eyes calmly observant.

She swallowed. "No, no. I'm fine," she lied, suppressing a sudden panic. What had happened to her just now?

"You looked as if you were going to faint."

His arm was heavy around her, and with his free hand he reached for her wrist to feel her pulse. She jerked her arm away. He was too close, much too close. Her heart was going berserk, hammering away frantically.

"I've never fainted in my life and I have no intention of starting now." She took a deep breath and straightened her spine, hoping he would take his arm away. He did not.

"I'd like another drink, please," she said, smelling his after-shave and the clean scent of soap and shampoo, feeling the warm weight of his arm against her bare shoulders. She was aware of a terrible contradiction of feelings—the clamoring need to feel him close, to be in his arms, and the fearful need to flee from him, to shake off his arm.

"I'll get you some water," he said.

"I want a drink. Gin and tonic." Her voice was a little shaky.

His eyes probed hers. "I think you've had enough."

Anger rushed through her at the implication of his words. "I said I'm fine!" she said in a fierce whisper. "You're not my doctor!" It sounded childish and it annoyed her. She shook herself free of his arm and stalked away, her legs trembling. In the bathroom she ran cold water over her wrists and put a wet towel against her heated cheeks. Her reflection was not reassuring. Her eyes were glittering feverishly and her face looked flushed.

This was the craziest thing that had ever happened to her. Something was definitely wrong with her. She was demented. The heat was curdling her brain.

If these women wanted Ross, they were welcome to him. He was an arrogant, infuriating male chauvinist, and they could have him, good looks, medical degree and all. She didn't need any of it, thank you very much.

She put on some more lipstick, fixed her hair and forced herself to relax. It was a luxurious bathroom, fitted with American fixtures and appliances in white and pale blue green, very cool and clean, a Western oasis of comfort.

She was just about to leave the oasis of comfort when a loud knocking came on the door. She opened it and found herself face to face with Ross, who scrutinised her in silence. She gritted her teeth.

"I said I'm all right."

"Just the same, I wasn't going to wait too long before finding out."

What if she hadn't answered? Would he have knocked down the door? The thought gave her a little thrill. No man had ever knocked in a door for her.

"I appreciate your concern," she said nicely, "but, as you can see, it's quite unnecessary. Now, may I pass, please?"

He was blocking her exit and he didn't move. "Just a minute. If you have any more of these . . . lapses, come into my office and let me check you out." He paused fractionally. "Or have Jay do it."

Have Ross check her out. As in taking off her clothes and letting him check her heartbeat, among other things. The thought sent her pulse racing. "*Or have Jay do it*," he had added, as if he had realized that a doctor-patient relationship with her might be a bit problematic. She pushed the images away.

"I had a complete physical just a month ago," she said as casually as possible. "I'm supremely healthy." There was nothing wrong with her except an unhealthy dose of jealousy, the unhappy realization of which had momentarily made her light-headed, but she could not very well explain that to him. Well, she could, of course, but she wasn't about to.

"Good," he said. "Now do yourself a favor and stay off the alcohol." He stepped aside to let her through and she moved into the party room and found herself another drink, a plain tonic with a slice of lemon. For a fraction of a moment she was tempted to flaunt a gin and tonic in front of him, but she knew it would only be a childish gesture. In her heart of hearts she had to admit she was touched by Ross's concern and, besides, she'd had two drinks already, and more would do her no good anyway. It would be much better if she could keep her wits about her.

As she brought the glass to her mouth, she saw Ross observing her only feet away, his eyes dark and unreadable.

"And how are you enjoying yourself?" Joe said at her side.

She turned to him and smiled, relieved to have her attention distracted from Ross. "This is wonderful—a little schizophrenic, though. I'm not sure I am in Africa."

"It's a schizophrenic life," he said, giving her a faint smile.

She could imagine. "I understand you are a man of two worlds. It can't be easy."

He gave her a long, assessing look. "No," he said then, "it isn't." He smiled. "But it has its rewards."

She liked him. He was personable and entertaining and she enjoyed talking to him about his life growing up in the little village not far out of Obalabi where his father was still the chief, about his experiences living and studying in the States. It was all in all the most interesting party she had ever attended.

She was going to have an interesting time here. And as long as Vicky was willing to put her up, there was no hurry to leave.

"What are you going to do with all that cloth?" Vicky asked the next day as she surveyed the growing stack of African print material in Sasha's room.

Sasha laughed. "I don't know yet. I'll think of something." She grinned to herself. She sure hoped she would. Her interest in the exotic fabric was close to becoming an obsession, yet she couldn't keep herself away from the shops and market stalls where they sold the stuff. Something was making her go back over and over again. Maybe there was a message in the compulsion. If so, it was time to find out.

Saamo had a sister who worked as a seamstress in a small sewing shop in town. Sasha sketched a picture of a simple, short shift dress, wrote in the measurements converted to metric and took over one of the pieces of market cloth.

With much gesturing and much laughing, and a little English, it was agreed that the dress would be made for her the very next day. It was an experiment of sorts. The shop was a small room with two barefoot young girls at two rather ancient-looking sewing machines. A rusty fan in the corner squeaked and squealed, blowing around odd scraps of fabric littering the bare concrete floor.

It took three days before the dress was finished, despite the ambitious promise of one, but it fitted her perfectly. The sewing skills could have been better, but it wasn't a bad job. The two girls watched her as she stood barefoot in front of a cracked mirror and examined her appearance. Apparently they found her dress rather amusing, and wondered why she wanted to use ordinary market cloth rather than the Western variety. Also, they were fascinated with her hair, wondering if she had dyed it. All of this caused rather a lot of hilarity, and Sasha was still smiling when she returned home with the dress.

Ross came over moments after she'd got in the door.

"I thought I'd let you know Jay is going to Accra the day after tomorrow," he said without preamble. "If you need a ride to the airport, you're welcome to go with him." His voice was cool, his eyes inscrutable as he watched her, hands in pockets, all casual, calm control.

"Are you still trying to get rid of me?" she asked.

"I'm offering you a ride," he said evenly.

She stared at him. "What do you have against me, Ross?"

He raised his dark brows. "Nothing, Auntie, nothing. I've just been wondering what you can possibly enjoy here doing nothing. Aren't you going crazy with boredom?"

She shrugged. "Not in the least. I'm having a terrific time."

"Reading books?"

"Absolutely." It seemed an incredible luxury to sit down with a book for an entire afternoon or evening and simply get lost in some new and fascinating world. In the last few years she'd been too busy to find much time for reading, something she'd always loved doing. "A lot of vicarious living is to be done by reading books." She smiled brightly. "I also enjoy shopping and getting to know the people. I like haggling with the market women."

"Don't you feel the necessity to do something useful with your time?"

Ah, the good doctor didn't like sloth and idleness. He was engaged in meaningful, rewarding work. It hurt his sensibilities to see her wasting away her time talking to market women and reading spy novels.

She shook her head. "Not in the least." She hadn't had a real vacation in three years; there'd never seemed to be time for more than a long weekend not too far away. She deserved some unadulterated lazing about. She felt no guilt whatsoever.

"When are you planning to leave?" he asked.

"I'm not. Planning, that is."

There was a loaded silence. The fan whirred briskly overhead. His eyes bored into hers. There was no friendly warmth there, no lights of humor.

"I want you out," he said then. No friendly warmth in his voice, either.

She nodded. "Yes, I gathered that. I am neither dumb nor deaf, Ross."

"You've had your visit. You've satisfied yourself that Vicky is doing fine. Now go back and tell her mother to stop worrying."

"I already did. I wrote her a letter."

"Have you given up your plans to take her back to the States?"

She gave a small smile. "I never had those plans, Doc. I have no idea where anybody got that notion."

His face tensed. "The notion came from Vicky's mother. She wrote she was sending you to pick her up."

She should have figured that out. Denise was a manipulator all right, but she'd known better than to ask Sasha straight out. She'd probably counted on her sister being appalled by what she would find and deciding on her own to convince Vicky to come home. Her schemes did not always work out. They certainly weren't now.

Sasha smiled at Ross. "Well, you should know by now—I'm not good at doing other people's bidding. And I don't like to be manipulated," she added meaningfully.

He ignored that. "So why are you still hanging around here?"

"Because I want to. I told you, I like it here. Is that so amazing? This is a fascinating place."

He looked skeptical. "Nobody wants to be here."

"No? You do. Jay and Nora do. Vicky does. Why not me?"

He cocked a mocking brow. "Doing what? Lazing away your time doing nothing?"

That really bothered him. She wondered why. "It seems to be hard for you to comprehend that what I do or do not do is absolutely none of your business. What's your agenda here, Doctor? Why do you want me out of the way so badly?"

His gaze was dark and inscrutable. "You have no business being here."

She shrugged. "Am I in the way? Do I interfere? Am I in any way a liability to you personally, or to the mission of this medical facility?"

His face went rigid. "I don't know what kind of game you're playing, but I warn you." He turned and strode out.

She let out a deep sigh. The little exchange had taken more out of her than she had expected. She felt exhausted. She sat down on the couch and stared mournfully at her hands lying in her lap. Nice hands, nice manicure. Perfect oval nails, polished misty berry. Definitely the hands of an idle, slothful person.

He didn't like her. He wanted her out of the way. It should make her angry, furious. Yet the odd thing was that it didn't. It did something very different. She sat still and stared at her nails, assessing the feeling, giving it a name.

She wasn't angry. She was hurt. And it wasn't easy to admit to the pain. And with the pain came the realization that she wanted him to see her, really see her, for what she was. When he looked at her he didn't see the woman she was; he saw someone very different. A parasite. A shiftless, out-of-work female looking for a good time.

It was her own fault. In the beginning she had played a game because he had made her angry. She'd not divested him of his illusions, not corrected his false assumptions.

Now he saw her as a frivolous nobody, doing nothing, taking life easy when all around her life was difficult and people worked hard for very little.

But she wasn't frivolous. She liked fun and laughter as much as the next guy, except perhaps Dr. Grant, who didn't seem to have any, but she also liked having an interesting job and working hard. As a matter of fact, she was excellent at working hard. So excellent, in fact, that in the past few years work had taken over her life, and fun and laughter had been left languishing by the wayside.

Now she was making up for lost time. Needless to say, however, one could not live by fun alone for an extended period. She had to admit that she had experienced a tiny twinge of restlessness in the last few days. It was an omen, a sign: it was time for new work, a new direction for her life.

Or maybe she should just pack up and go to Kenya and go on her safari as she had planned.

No. She didn't want to leave Obalabi. Life here was a challenge. She thrived on challenge. She was aware of a sense of expectation, of something waiting to happen. It was a very exciting feeling, the kind you had when you were little and waiting to open an enormous, intriguing birthday present. There was a mysterious, possibly divine voice inside her telling her to stay in Obalabi, to be patient.

Patient for what?

She couldn't wait to find out.

Sasha had noticed that the posters in the under-fives clinic left a lot to be desired in terms of general cheer and color. With Vicky's blessing, she set out to do something about it. Having time on her hands and being handy with pen and paint, Sasha revamped the posters with flair and style.

In essence the posters were the same. She had no intention of messing with the message. She had added bright color and whimsical touches—a plumed crimson bird, a small emerald green frog with a human face, a cobalt and orange fish leaping from a stream.

They might not be great pieces of art, but they were fun, and they certainly elicited laughter from the women and children visiting the clinic. They elicited a long, silent observation from Ross when he walked in the day she was hanging up the last one.

"You did this?" he asked.

"Yes." She could not tell anything from his tone—whether he liked the posters or not. "I thought a little frivolity wouldn't do any harm." She offered him a sunny smile. "I do so like to spread a little cheer," she added for good measure.

He threw her a rather obscure look, then moved on to the next poster and scrutinized it. She saw the smile tug at his mouth. The satisfaction she felt seemed quite out of proportion. It made her a little light in the head. He turned to look at her, pushing his hands into the pockets of his white coat.

"I like what you did with them. The other ones were rather drab and unimaginative."

"Thank you. I'm glad you approve."

He glanced at his watch, his mind on loftier matters again, then marched out of the room. Off to his meeting with the visiting health department officials from Burkino Faso, who wanted to look at the way this GHO hospital functioned. Obalabi hospital, as a small, rural facility, was a success story, due, according to Vicky, to Ross's innovative management skills as well as his creative medical talents. Ross was a paragon.

Sasha watched his broad back as he strode down the breezeway and smiled.

How about that? she thought. We actually had a civilized exchange of words. He actually approved of something I did. Something fun and frivolous at that. It seemed at that moment a small miracle.

She felt a grin spread on her face. And, somewhere in the far recesses of her mind, a tiny spark began to glow.

Several days later, a bright idea hit her in the middle of the night—a vision of much color and clarity.

She sat up in bed, her heart pounding, adrenaline flowing, wondering if she were actually awake. She pinched herself hard and winced. She was awake. She needed a pen, paper, lots of paper. She needed coffee for a clear head.

It's three o'clock! You're *crazy*!

So what else was new? She scrambled out of bed, carefully opening her door so that it wouldn't creak, and tiptoed down the hall, past Vicky's room, to the kitchen to make herself some of the toxic instant coffee. While she waited for the water to boil, she ate a banana and foraged for pencil, paper and calculator. There was a tiny solar-powered one inside her wallet.

She sat at the wobbly dining room table and drew pictures, made calculations and projections. In a short time the table was littered with designs for dresses, skirts, shorts and tops, littered with papers full of numbers and dollar signs.

No, she couldn't do this. It was much too ambitious a project. There were a thousand things involved that she didn't know a thing about. She'd only been here a short time—she didn't know how things operated here. She was on vacation.

Where there is a will there is a way.

She could ask Joe Doranga for advice.

If she could find enough people with enough sewing machines... She could *buy* sewing machines if she had to, and start her own sewing shop.

But first she needed to start small, with a sample line, just to try it out. She needed to send them to Caroline and see if she was willing to sell the exotic African print clothes in La Très Chic Boutique Antique.

She gathered the papers into a pile, then got up and made another cup of coffee and took it to the couch. Drawing up her knees to her chin, she sat and reflected. It was necessary to digest everything for a while. Not to jump too fast.

A knock on the door startled her. People didn't come knocking at four-thirty in the morning. Unless it was a witch in search of someone's soul for a late-night snack. Oh, stop it, she told herself. She unfolded herself from the couch and went to the door. "Who is it?" she asked.

"Ross," came the short reply.

Ross. Her heart did a somersault. She unlocked the door and opened it, realizing that she was barefoot and wearing nothing but a thin white cotton nightgown. Well, he spent his waking life looking at people in their nightclothes. He stepped inside and glanced around.

"Where's Vicky? Is she all right?"

"Of course she's all right. She's asleep."

He frowned and ran a weary hand through his hair. He looked exhausted. "Why are you up at this hour?" he asked.

I was having a vision.

"I couldn't sleep. And what are you doing prowling through the compound at night?"

"I was at the hospital. There was an emergency." He rubbed his neck and his eyes looked dull. She needn't have worried about wearing nothing but a shorty nightgown. He wasn't seeing her at all. Which was just as well. The nightgown was lovely, if a bit wrinkled, but her face was bare of makeup and her hair was standing on end like a ragged red brush. She was not exactly a picture of female loveliness.

"Would you like a cup of coffee? Or a drink?" she asked generously, taking pity on him. The man had been working in the middle of the night, and it didn't look as if he'd been having a very good time.

He checked his watch. "Coffee. It's too late to go back to bed."

"Sit," she said, waving at a chair. "I'll be right back."

She heated water and poured it on the coffee granules. It foamed disgustingly. She stirred the mugs, then carried them back to the living room.

"What kind of emergency?" she asked, handing him a cup. "What happened?"

"A young woman. She's dying. I don't know why." His voice was toneless.

She frowned. "Dying? Just like that?"

"Oh, no, not just like that. But I don't know the cause. We can't find a single reason why she should be dying, only she is. All the lab work comes out negative. All the tests are normal." His face grew rigid with frustration and he slammed his fist into the palm of his other hand. "Damn it! It's the third one in the last few months."

This did not sound like an uplifting story.

"The third one? What's going on?"

"Juju. That's what the relatives say. Unfortunately, we have not yet developed an antidote for juju."

She felt a shiver go down her spine. "What do you think happened?"

He took a swallow of the coffee and grimaced at the taste of it. "There are two possibilities," he said. "One, it's a case of self-fulfilling prophesy. The patient believes a spell has been put on him and that he's going to die. So he does. Or she, as the case may be."

"Just like that?"

"Mind over matter. Autosuggestion. The mind is very powerful. The second possibility is poisoning. I imagine people here can cook up lethal potions never encountered by modern science. We have no way to test for them. They don't show up in the lab work and there you go, a mysterious death. And again an affirmation that juju is more powerful than Western medicine."

Obviously, this did not enthral him one bit. He was a man of science. He didn't like to fight hocus-pocus and then lose. He didn't like to feel helpless. But then, who did?

"Have some more coffee," she said consolingly.

He looked at his cup in distaste. "This stuff is noxious. I don't understand why Vicky insists on buying it."

"What choice is there?" The shops in Obalabi offered only instant, and then only one brand. It had a label that promised energy, vitality and a long life.

Drip coffee, he said. He was not a man who craved many luxuries, but a good cup of coffee was sacred. On his occasional forays into Ouagadougou, he stocked up on the real thing, which was then brewed in his imported electric drip coffeemaker, either by himself, or his trusty servant Youssouf.

So he liked good coffee. "What is your favorite meal?" she asked on impulse.

"A thick, juicy steak," he said without hesitation. "With a baked potato with sour cream, a green salad with Roquefort dressing and garlic bread with large quantities of butter."

She groaned. "God, didn't they teach you about cholesterol in medical school?"

"I went sailing that day."

She laughed. "What's your favorite dessert?"

He grinned. "Cheesecake, what else?"

"Are you serious?"

"Deadly. Why else do you think I live here? At home I'd eat myself to death."

She made a face. "I can see that. Lack of self-discipline is a dangerous character fault." Which was rather a joke. If she'd ever seen anyone with self-discipline, it was Ross Grant.

"And what about you?" he asked.

"I don't think we should be doing this," she said, giving him a pained expression. "It's making me hungry."

"Maybe we should have breakfast. Eggs Benedict with sausages on the side."

"You have a sick mind," she said and got up. "I'm going to make some more coffee and have a banana. How about you?"

He grimaced. "I changed my mind about the drink. Do you have anything less lethal than that coffee?"

"There's gin. Also there's some German schnapps that Jochen left here."

"Schnapps sounds perfect."

She abandoned the thought of coffee herself and had some schnapps as well. They talked easily for a while and she found out that he had lost his parents at an early age and that he and his brother Jake had been brought up by their maternal grandparents, avid sailors and generally positive folks who embraced life with cheerfulness and enthusiasm.

She listened, aware that something quite special was happening: Ross was talking about himself. He seemed relaxed now and his earlier moroseness had vanished. He was showing her a different side of himself. He was . . . approachable.

She decided to seize the opportunity and ask him some probing questions, questions that might reveal something more about the secret inner world hiding behind his normally remote demeanor.

"What do you miss most living in Obalabi?" she asked.

"Water," he said promptly, taking another swallow of schnapps.

Water. She frowned. It was not terribly revealing, at least not that she could see. "Water such as the kind you drink? The kind that falls from the sky? The kind that churns in rivers?" All these were in short supply in Obalabi.

"As in oceans, seas and lakes," said Ross. "I like swimming and sailing. Very therapeutic exercise."

Sasha could only agree.

They discovered, over the course of an hour and two glasses of schnapps, that they had in common, in addition to a love of swimming and sailing, a passion for classic Spanish guitar, smelly cheeses, and saunas. None of these, unfortunately, was available in Obalabi. They both professed a loathing for red beets, steel-and-chrome furniture, and the Grateful Dead. Fortunately, none of these was available in Obalabi, either.

It all was very promising. There was a sudden closeness, a lifting of hostilities that was most comforting to Sasha. Apart from the steady drone of insects outside, the world was very quiet. It seemed, in some odd way, that they were all alone in the world and whatever problems and conflicts there had been were wiped out by the darkness of the night.

It was nice to see him smile. It was nice that she was able to make him smile. He was like a different man. Or at least he displayed a different side of his personality, a more relaxed, humorous side to which she found it easy to relate. She also found that it stirred in her distinctly disturbing feelings, feelings that made her slightly light-headed. The atmosphere was electric.

"There's another thing I like," he said. "Red hair." He reached out his hand and let it trail through her curls. The warm glow inside her suddenly burst into flame.

"Me too," she said, her voice a little husky. She'd even liked it as a little girl, because it was different and people were always commenting on it. She'd gloried in the admiration. Most of her friends had had some nondistinct shade of mousy brown or dirty blonde, except for her little Korean friend Hae-Joo, who'd had shiny black hair and very interesting eyes. It was the only time she remembered being briefly envious of someone else's hair and eyes.

And here she was on a sofa in Africa with a man caressing her hair, saying he loved it. Her heart was beating rather frantically and her blood was singing. His hand kept moving through her hair, slowly, rhythmically, and she found it suddenly difficult to breathe. Her body was oddly trembly and she fixed her eyes desperately on her hands in her lap, afraid to meet his.

His other hand lifted her chin and she had no choice but to look into his eyes. It was almost a shock to see them—deep and dark and full of a brooding passion.

His hand stilled on her hair. They gazed at each other for long, tense moments, the air vibrating around them.

It took no effort at all to move toward him. No effort at all to slip her arms around him. She'd craved his closeness, the warmth of his body against hers. Her mind had denied it, her heart had not.

His kiss was like an explosion. Her head was full of stars, her body full of fire.

"Oh, God, Sasha," he muttered hoarsely. "This is madness . . ."

It was madness and she didn't care. It was what she wanted, needed. Her heart cried out for him.

His hands roamed over her body, moving under her nightgown and caressing her breasts. All thought vanished and all was emotion and need and pure pleasure. His touch made her senses dance, her nerves tingle.

He let her go abruptly and she gave a small moan of protest. She opened her eyes, dragging herself back to reality. Her breathing was shallow and she glanced over at Ross, feeling bereft. He was leaning back against the sofa, his eyes closed as if in deep pain.

"I apologize," he said at last, his voice strained. "I shouldn't have let this happen."

She stared at him, her heart still racing. "There's no need to apologize," she said lightly. "I'm not offended."

He said nothing, his face a mask showing no emotion, his eyes empty.

Fear ran like ice through her blood. "Ross, what's wrong?" she whispered.

"Nothing." He shook his head as if to clear his thoughts. "Nothing." He came to his feet and moved to the door.

She felt rooted to the sofa, unable to move. She looked at his empty face, still feeling his kiss hot on her mouth, and she felt a flare of anger mixed with despair. Was it so terrible to kiss me? she wanted to ask, but pride kept the words inside.

He left without a word.

In the next few days it became obvious that whatever had transpired on that night had nothing to do with reality. It had taken place in another sphere of consciousness. Ross was trying to avoid her. When this failed and he had no choice but to spend time in her presence he was remote and polite. Her emotions were a simmering stew of anger, hurt, bafflement and humiliation, but the greatest of these was anger, a smoldering anger that poisoned her mood even as she worked on her clothing project.

Why was he rejecting her? What was so terrible about kissing her? Why was he acting as if he wanted nothing to do with her?

Oh, damn him. What did she care? She didn't want him. Somehow it was important that she convince herself of this. Her pride was at stake here.

How she did it, she wasn't even sure, but two weeks later she had a small sample collection of shift dresses, long skirts and tops, short skirts and tops, all made of various African print fabric.

Vicky loved them. Christine loved them. Nora loved them. Getting them to the States was no problem, Nora said. She and Jay were going on home leave in three days and she'd carry them back with her and make sure they'd end up at La Très Chic Boutique Antique.

"But it's not old stuff," Vicky said irreverently. The old stuff she was referring to was exquisite, expensive clothing from magic eras gone by. Vicky, apparently, had no understanding of the true nature of the lovely merchandise sold by the boutique.

"No," said Sasha, "this isn't old stuff. But it's *different*. It's *exotic*. People in New York are always looking for something different."

"Does Caroline want to carry it?"

"She said she'll start a sideline." She'd been able, after several attempts, to get a phone call through to Caroline. "And if it becomes a rage, I can start another store. La Très Chic Boutique Exotique." And why not? Dreaming big was fun. Having visions of grandeur was fun.

"It's not going to be easy," Vicky said. "Things here don't work the way you're used to. Everything takes a long time."

There was a silence. They looked at each other, aware that they were thinking the same thing.

"I want to ask you something," Sasha said slowly. "And I'd like an honest answer."

"I know," said Vicky. "And the answer is yes. You can stay as long as you like."

"Are you sure?"

Vicky nodded. "I like having you here, you know I do, and I think what you're trying to do is important. I mean, if it works it might help create jobs here and bring some money to people who need it."

It certainly sounded very lofty. And if doing good works was fun, why not? However, raising hopes too soon would not be advantageous for anybody.

"I can't promise anything," Sasha said carefully. "It's only an idea at this point. I don't know if it's going to work, but I'd like to give it a try."

"So give it a try. Stay."

Three weeks later, she received a telegram from Caroline sent to her at the hospital, saying more than half the samples had been sold, and to please send more as soon as possible. Especially the short shift dresses and the long skirts were popular. "SEND WHATEVER YOU CAN ASAP!"

* * *

As she raced around the dusty streets of Obalabi from sewing shop to sewing shop getting more clothes made, Sasha was doing a lot of thinking. People were poor here. Farming was bad, and much other work simply wasn't available. Starting a cottage industry would make a difference to some of the families in Obalabi. The idea gave her a warm, fuzzy feeling of satisfaction. The work would be done here and the money for that work could come from a place where people had it to spend: the clients of La Très Chic Boutique Antique. Most of them had more money than they knew what to do with. She might as well help them put some of it to good use.

It was a very exciting idea. She would be doing what she was good at: using her business talents to do something that would make a difference. All by herself she would help redistribute a little of the world's wealth, the problem much debated by economists and politicians while sitting in plush offices. And here she was, Sasha LeClerc, not debating, but doing. It was a heady thought.

It was a terrifying thought. Twice she woke up at night, swimming in perspiration and doubt. Fortunately, she managed to get herself in hand. She was a practical, down-to-earth person. She knew what she was doing. There was nothing to worry about. She'd started a business up from the ground once. She would do it again.

"You will go on a far journey and find your destiny," the gypsy had said. Well, maybe this was her destiny. Why not?

She would find out soon enough if it were true, if she could make it work.

* * *

It was Tuesday morning and she awoke early, just past six. She always awoke at dawn, and for a few minutes she would lie still and listen to the peaceful sounds of birds and the chickens coming from the mud hut compound she could see from her window. It was cool, a bracing, delicious cool that would not last long. The fierce sun conquered it with merciless force, and fast.

She heard Vicky stir around, getting ready for work, and Sasha leaped out of bed and went into the bathroom to shower, hearing Saamo moving around in the kitchen getting their breakfast ready.

As she came out of the bathroom a while later, a draught blew across the hall and Vicky's bedroom door flew open. Dressed in white panties and bra, Vicky stood in the middle of the room, looking frail and thin. She turned in surprise as the door hit the wall.

"Good morning," Sasha said, reaching for the door to close it again. But her arm stopped in midair and her body froze at the frightful sight of what Vicky was doing.

CHAPTER FIVE

SASHA forgot to breathe. She stared at Vicky, who looked back at her with huge gray eyes. The silence quivered with tension.

Vicky stood rigid, a hypodermic needle in her hand which only moments before she'd carefully taken out of her arm. Sasha took in a deep breath. Terrifying visions, thoughts and fears ran rampant in her head. Was Vicky taking drugs? Was that why she was acting so strangely at times? Was that the reason for the weight loss?

"Vicky?" she whispered. "What are you doing?"

Vicky stirred into movement, turned her back and slipped the needle into a plastic container. "You saw what I was doing," she said tightly. "And it's none of your business."

"Vicky!" Sasha rushed into the room and caught Vicky's arm. "I don't care if it's my business or not! What did you just give yourself? Tell me!"

Vicky shook herself free and slowly sank down on the bed. Her face crumpled.

"I suppose I might as well tell you," she said dully. "You're going to find out sooner or later anyway." She swallowed. "It was insulin."

"*Insulin*?" Sasha wasn't sure if she was relieved or shocked.

"I've got diabetes." Vicky clenched her hands in her lap.

Sasha's heart contracted. "Oh, Vicky," she whispered, "I'm so sorry."

Vicky jumped to her feet. "It's not fatal, for heaven's sake! Don't look at me like that!" She was struggling for composure and dignity, which was not a feat easily accomplished standing in your underwear.

"Vicky, diabetes is serious!"

Vicky yanked her pink flowered robe off a hook, pulled it on and parked her hands on her bony hips. Her clear silvery eyes looked Sasha squarely in the face. "I am an intelligent, trained medical professional. Don't tell me my business! And now, if you'll excuse me, I need to get dressed so I can go to work."

"We need to talk about this, Vicky."

"No, we don't." Vicky turned her pink flowered back with finality.

Sasha left the room and carefully closed the door, feeling numb with shock.

At breakfast Vicky pretended nothing was wrong, keeping up a constant stream of inane chatter until Sasha was ready to scream at her. She managed to contain it and concentrated on her bread and scrambled guinea-fowl eggs. She was relieved when Vicky finally left for the hospital.

Everything was falling into place. The weight loss, the wary, guarded expressions on Vicky's face. The cookies. The damned cookies! Ross's sharp question. "You did what?" And later, "Are there any more of these? She doesn't eat much sweet stuff any more... Hand them over, Auntie." He'd eaten practically an entire bag of fig bars so she wouldn't have them to give to Vicky, and then he'd been ready to eat another. He hadn't wanted Vicky to be tempted. He hadn't known about the big can of chocolate chip cookies hiding in her suitcase as well. The same can that had later been dessert for the neighborhood at dinner. And then she remembered Daniella: "She's doing just fine, you know... Ross and Jay are looking after her."

And then another, more recent memory. Ross knocking on the door in the middle of the night when she'd been up dealing with her vision. He'd inquired where Vicky was, and how she was doing.

She closed her eyes. They were all worried she would find out, worried she might convince Vicky to go home to the States. But Vicky was needed here; they didn't want her to leave. Where else would they find a good nursing teacher willing to live in Obalabi? Many nurses were ordinary women repulsed by ordinary bugs and requiring ordinary comforts such as a clean supermarket for their food and a beauty salon for their perms. Vicky had no particular feelings toward bugs, be they ordinary or exotic. Her naturally curly hair did not require perms and she was happy with a random cut of freshly slaughtered goat from the open-air market.

They wanted Vicky right where she was: in Obalabi.

Sasha felt a growing outrage. Indignation clogged her throat. Her body temperature rose alarmingly. Damn Ross!

She was going to confront him and she wasn't going to wait until he got home. Her anger needed venting now. Ross made his rounds at eight; she'd corner him before that.

She waited in the doctors' lounge while a nurse went to find him. Her body was too tense to sit, so she paced up and down restlessly. She didn't have to wait long. Ross entered the room, dressed in surgical green, and her heart lurched.

Amazing how attractive a man could look wearing a shapeless garment of the medical variety. He looked big and imposing, his dark eyes questioning.

"Good morning," he said. "Is there a problem?"

"Yes," she said tightly.

He eyed her with academic interest. "Something wrong?"

She clenched her hands. "Yes."

"So spit it out." He crossed his arms in front of his chest and waited.

"I've finally discovered why you were so worried about me talking Vicky into going back to the States. I couldn't imagine why you thought I could do that. Well, I know now!"

He cocked a dark brow. "You do?"

It took an effort to stay calm. "She has diabetes."

"So she does." Cool as a cucumber he was. Of course, along with all the exotic tropical ailments he dealt with, diabetes was merely a run-of-the-mill boring disease. Nothing much to get excited about.

"You should have told me!"

His brows rose in sardonic amusement. "I should have told you? I am her doctor. I do not discuss my patients with outsiders without their consent. However, I did tell Vicky that in my professional opinion this sort of thing is much better off in the open. I suggested she tell you, but she didn't want to. It was not my place to inform you against her wishes."

"You should have told her to go home!"

Again the sardonic look. "Is that your professional medical opinion?"

"You don't want her to go, do you? You want her to stay for your own selfish reasons! You're despicable!"

His eyes darkened dangerously. He took a step toward her. He was too close for comfort, but she refused to budge. She anchored her feet to the floor and stared straight back into his face. He was not going to intimidate her because of his size.

There was a loaded silence. "Are you telling me," he said, his voice soft and dangerous, "that my medical ethics leave something to be desired? Are you questioning my medical professionalism?"

Her legs were shaking. "Yes, I am!" She turned in what she hoped was a dignified manner and marched out of the room, back into the hot sunshine. Blindly she made her way back to the house.

What was she going to do now? Her fury, swept high for a couple of hours, was dissipating. Another feeling was replacing it. Disillusionment. Wild and bitter.

Ross wasn't the dedicated, caring doctor she'd thought he was. He was using Vicky. He should have sent her back to the States. Her opinion of him as a man left a lot to be desired; her opinion of him as a physician was exalted. *Had been*. It now lay shattered like delicate crystal.

Shortly after noon, Vicky came home for lunch, and her expression, as she walked in the door, promised nothing good.

"You went to see Ross," she stated, her voice barely controlled.

"Did he tell you?"

"No, he did not tell me. I saw you come out of the doctors' lounge and by the way you were walking I could tell what had been going on in there. You had no right!"

"I think it's unconscionable that they didn't send you home!"

Vicky's eyes shot fire. "I was given the choice! And it was *my* decision! I decided to stay because there wasn't any reason not to!"

"How can you say that?"

"Where would I be safer than right here? I am a nurse and I know how to take care of myself. I work all day in a hospital and I have two very good doctors watching over me like a pair of hawks. Do you think for a moment either Ross or Jay would allow me to stay if I put myself at risk here? How can you even *think* that?"

Vicky didn't wait for an answer. She stalked out of the house without eating lunch, no doubt to share the midday meal with the nurses.

All afternoon Sasha kept thinking of Vicky, about Denise's premonition that something wasn't right. Vicky hadn't told her mother she'd developed diabetes, but a sixth sense or her intuition had told Denise something was wrong.

Vicky's words kept coming back to her over and over again. Now that her anger had subsided and reason was claiming its rightful territory she was beginning to wonder if her concern for Vicky wasn't overdone. What Vicky had said made perfect sense. Where could she be safer than right here with two doctors taking a personal interest in her well-being?

"Do you think for a moment either Ross or Jay would allow me to stay if I put myself at risk here?"

Sasha was beginning to feel like a first-class fool about her hotheaded confrontation with Ross that morning. She regretted upsetting Vicky.

It wasn't difficult making up with Vicky when she came home that afternoon. Vicky didn't like being angry. She'd rather have peace and serenity, love and good cheer.

Apologizing to Ross would not be so easy.

Oh, God. Sasha groaned and buried her face in her hands. She was sitting on the edge of her bed, gathering courage. Dinner was over. Ross was home now. She should go to see him and do what had to be done, like a responsible, mature person.

After all, fair was fair. She owed him an apology. She had said, for all intents and purposes, that he was unethical. Not a minor accusation. Not one that would simply be forgotten.

Dignity was what she needed. She rose from the bed and straightened her spine. She glanced down at her clothes. Loose black harem trousers, gathered at the ankles. A sleeveless top of honey-colored silk. She found a long scarf with a leafy design in black and various shades of gold and brown and tied it around her waist. She brushed her hair, put on fresh lipstick, lifted her chin and swept out of the room. She walked to his house and knocked on the door.

He opened the door himself. He was dressed in pale cotton pants and a colorful shirt, open at the neck. His face was inscrutable as he looked at her. "What can I do for you?" he asked coolly.

"I need a doctor," she said.

One dark brow quirked. "I'm off duty. I'll be happy to see you in the morning."

"It can't wait."

"I see. It's serious, then."

"Yes." Her gaze did not waver. She was not about to be sent away now.

"Well, come in, then." He waved at a chair. "Sit down."

She sat down.

His house was much the same as Vicky's. The dining room table at the far end of the room was covered with papers. He must have been working.

He lowered himself in a chair across from her, leaned back and crossed his arms in front of his chest. "So what's the problem?"

She took a deep breath. "I'm suffering from a serious case of bad conscience."

He nodded slowly, as if this did not surprise him. "I see."

It was all he said, and it was not promising. He wanted her to squirm. Maybe she deserved to squirm. However, squirming wasn't one of her talents and she'd try to avoid it if she could. "Do you have any pills that might help?" she asked lightly. "Or any kind of magic potion?"

"No," he said.

This was not going well. "You're a doctor. Aren't you supposed to ask me questions about my symptoms?"

"What are your symptoms?" he asked obligingly.

She put her hand on her breast. "Chest pains. A tight feeling in my stomach. Headache. I keep wincing and calling myself unflattering names."

He nodded. "Classical." He rose to his feet. "Wait." He disappeared, coming back a moment later carrying two glasses. He handed her one. "This might help a little. It's not a cure, unfortunately, only a temporary relief of the symptoms."

"Thank you." She took a sip of the Scotch, then took another deep breath and called forth all the dignity she could muster and looked him squarely in the eyes.

"I want to apologize for my outburst this morning, and—er—my attack on your integrity." Her heart was pounding so loud that she was afraid he might hear it. "It was uncalled for and I regret my loss of temper and perspective."

So there, she'd done it. And nicely, too. A proper, mature, adult apology. She took another gulp of her drink and promptly choked. She coughed and sputtered, spraying whisky over her harem pants. A cloth napkin was tossed into her lap and she heard Ross laugh out loud.

Well, there went her dignity. She mopped herself up with fatalistic resignation and placed both glass and napkin on the table, not looking at him. Silence reigned. She looked at the wall. A minute passed and it was still silent in the room. She could not keep looking at the wall forever; she'd have to meet his eyes sooner or later, so she finally did, seeing the humor lurking in their dark depths, a grin still on his face.

"You've got class, Auntie," he said. "Real class."

"Oh, be quiet! And don't call me Auntie! I apologize and all you do is laugh!" She bit her lip, and then she was laughing too.

"Apology accepted. How are you feeling now?"

"Cured, quite cured. You're a miracle worker."

"I'm glad I could be of service, even at this late hour."

She came to her feet. "I appreciate it. Send me the bill, Doc."

He opened the door for her. "It's on the house."

They stood close together, eyes locked, and suddenly her feet wouldn't move.

"You smell like a lush," he said, his mouth curving.

"Now that's a compliment I haven't heard before. You sure know how to make a woman feel good." The words had popped out of their own accord. At least, she thought so. Surely she had more sense than to give him a challenge like that?

For a moment there was absolute stillness. She looked at him, and the breath stuck in her throat. The air was charged with a quivering energy. Something flickered in his eyes, a brief struggle, a flash point instantly burned out. Then he was kissing her, deep and hungrily, his arms drawing her so tight against his chest that she could barely breathe. For a moment it seemed he had lost all restraint, then he eased his hold on her, sliding his hands upward and burying them in her hair, cradling her head. His kiss now was full of a deep sensuality and she found her emotions reeling. A soft moan escaped her and the kiss intensified again, his tongue playing an erotic game with hers.

She was lost; hopelessly, totally lost. A deep yearning warmed her body and she trembled against him. Her arms went around him, holding on to him as if she were a drowning victim. Her heart was pounding against her ribs. His body against hers was warm and solid and she felt in the grip of an overwhelming desire. She answered his kiss with a passion of her own, not caring now about anything but the fire between them.

He was an expert, no doubt about it, yet his kiss and the way he touched her were anything but studied and mechanical. It was pure, primal pleasure.

Then he released her and it took her a moment to descend back to earth, to feel the ground solidify under her feet.

"How do you feel now?" he asked, observing her with a half smile.

Gathering composure to answer his question took considerable effort. Her legs were shaking and she leaned against the wall, crossing her arms in front of her chest in a pose of studied calm. She met his challenge with a smile of her own. "I have to admit, you're good, real good."

"Thank you," he said with a gracious bow of his head.

She pushed herself away from the wall and made for the door. "Well, I'd better be going. Good night."

"Good night."

She took a deep, shuddering breath as she walked back to Vicky's house, amazed at her presence of mind after he'd stopped kissing her. Amazed that she'd actually walked out of his house. Going home wasn't at all what she had wanted.

Ross Grant knew how to make a woman feel good.

Vicky looked up absently from her book as Sasha came back into the room. "Where did you go? You kind of disappeared on me."

"Oh, I—er—I went to Ross to apologize."

"That took you quite a while."

Sasha sagged into a chair and shrugged. "We had a drink."

"How about that," Vicky said dryly.

"What's wrong with that?"

"Nothing, except that the two of you don't spend any more time in each other's company than is absolutely necessary." She eyed Sasha shrewdly. "Do I see signs of truce negotiations?"

Sasha got up from the chair. "Read your book."

Vicky laughed.

Sasha didn't see Ross the next day. She even missed seeing him walk past the window as she had her first cup of coffee. She admitted to herself that she was disappointed. He must have gone to the hospital very early. Maybe he had lain awake all night thinking about her, and, being unable to sleep, had left early.

Fat chance.

Later that morning she stopped by the hospital on some pretext, hoping to run into him. It was immature and foolish, and also unsuccessful, and she went home, feeling deflated.

She was in love, no doubt about it. It made no sense to deny it. It made her feel shaky and excited.

She was in love with Ross, with his eyes, his mouth when he smiled, his gentle hands, his hair that fell over his forehead, his mouth, strong and sensual, made for kissing. She was in love with his long-legged stride, with his gravelly voice and his crooked smile. She liked listening to his stories. She loved seeing him in his white doctor's coat, or his shapeless surgery greens which seemed very sexy to her. Now that she had embraced the truth herself, she wanted the situation to move forward.

As the days passed, she felt herself grow increasingly morose. Nothing in Ross's behavior gave any indication that the few wild moments of passion they had shared that night had affected him in any way at all. When they were together, he treated her as casually as he did the others. No secret little smile, no squeeze of her hand, no touch of her hair. The kiss, apparently, had not been a great moment of revelation. He had not finally admitted to himself that he wanted her. And he did, didn't he? Her instincts told her he did. His actions didn't bear this out. He was certainly not actively pursuing her.

She wanted to be pursued.

It was not easy to take. Sasha had to admit to herself that she was not used to men who showed so very little interest in her when it was obvious she was interested in them. It wasn't good for her ego. It was worse for her heart. At night she lay in bed, unable to sleep, wondering about her feelings for Ross, wondering what to do. She could not figure him out. There was all this passion in him, yet he seemed determined to keep it all locked up inside him, hidden behind that apparently cool, uninterested facade he showed her.

Even in the daytime while she was busy putting her plan to work she thought of him constantly. The days went by and nothing happened. Ross was politely friendly, which was an improvement of sorts. He seemed to have given up trying to get rid of her and she felt comforted by the thought. Maybe she should just play it by ear. Well, what other choice did she have?

Her business started rolling like a train. She found several more women to do the sewing, women who were willing to follow her instructions and learn to do the sewing the way she wanted it done. Joe and his wife came to town for a traditional ceremony and Sasha went to see him in his fancy house and asked him for advice. With the welfare of his people close to his heart, Joe was more than willing to help. He had many contacts and many relatives. Within two days she had an ambitious and educated sister working for her, a pretty young woman who was eager to put her business talents to work. Fatima would help to develop the business, then take it over when Sasha eventually left the country. It was a wonderful plan.

There was, of course, the matter of Sasha being a foreigner in the country. The matter of licenses and permits, of illegal business activities, of deportation and the possibility of languishing in an African jail. With this, too, Joe offered help. Contracts were drawn up and papers signed. It was all working out splendidly.

Joe offered more help. If she could see to it that the boxed clothing was delivered to his office in Accra, he would take care of the shipping to the States until a more regular routine could be worked out. He saw to the purchase of six sewing machines for her in Accra and had them shipped to Obalabi.

They arrived by truck late one afternoon, just as Ross was coming home from the hospital.

"What is this?" Ross asked, seeing the driver unload the sewing machines.

"Sewing machines," she said promptly and gave him a bright smile.

"For what?"

"For sewing."

"What are you up to?"

"I've started a little business in town making dresses and skirts."

"A little business? Are you out of your mind?"

"No, not that I'm aware of." She smiled at the driver and paid him some extra money for his help. He grinned at her and leaped back into the truck.

Ross took her arm and practically dragged her into the house, nearly tripping over the neat piles of blouses and dresses and skirts. He stopped dead, staring at the colorful display on the floor, his hand still painful on her arm.

"What the hell is going on here?" His voice was low and dangerous.

"I have employed twelve women part-time for six months to sew clothes. You were concerned about my not doing anything useful, so I thought perhaps I'd better do something useful."

"And what are you planning to do with these clothes?"

"Sell them in the States."

He glanced around. "Quite the entrepreneur, are you?"

"It's in the blood, they tell me."

"Just because you had a successful business in the States that doesn't mean you can start one here."

So he knew about La Très Chic Boutique Antique. Well, he was a smart man. He probably had figured out she wasn't exactly what he'd thought and made a few inquiries.

"If I don't try, I won't find out, will I?" She stacked some of the clothes in a box, then picked up another pile.

"You know how many schemes like this fail every year? Do you know what happens to these women after you leave and the work is gone?"

"I considered that, yes."

"What are you going to say to them when you leave? 'I've made myself a buck, thanks a lot. I'm going now?' " His eyes were furious, his voice hard. "Don't you understand what you are doing? You're raising expectations! They're going to count on this little venture to continue! You're being selfish and greedy at the expense of these women!"

She glared at him, furious. "Maybe I'm not so stupid that I don't understand that," she said slowly. "Maybe it's time you should credit me with some brains and insight. Maybe," she said even slower, looking right into his angry eyes, "I don't plan on leaving." At least not for a while. She wasn't leaving until she was sure Fatima was ready for her to leave.

He gave a dry, mocking laugh "Oh, you'll leave, don't make a mistake about it. It may be fun and exciting now, but it won't last long, believe me." He turned and walked off.

Why did he dislike her so? She looked at the piles of clothes and the colors blurred before her eyes.

She sank down on the couch, body tense, fighting tears.

And why did the tears come so easily when she thought about him? Why was she always longing for his arms around her?

After dinner that night she went to his house to ask for a novel she'd wanted to read. It was a pretext to see him, and she had no illusions that he'd recognize it as such. What she wanted was an answer to a question that had been on her mind too long.

"I was wondering if you'd finished the Clancy book," she said when he opened the door.

He gave her an assessing look. "I have. Come in and I'll get it."

She stood in the living room while he left to get it from his bedroom. He handed it to her, not offering her a seat or a drink. She felt distinctly unwelcome.

She stared at the book, gathering courage, then raised her gaze to meet his. "Tell me something." She felt oddly light-headed and it seemed suddenly a big effort to keep talking. If she asked the question, she would get an answer. She might not like the answer.

Well, she was a big girl. She could take it. She squared her shoulders. "Tell me, why do you hate me so?"

He grew very still, as if the question came as a shock to him. His eyes locked with hers. His jaw worked, and for an instant she saw a strange emotion flit across his features. Despair? Fear?

She must have imagined it. She blinked. When she looked again, his face was cool and composed.

"I don't hate you," he said.

CHAPTER SIX

"THEN what do you have against me? You know I'm not trying to convince Vicky to go back to the States, so what is it?"

"You don't belong here," he said.

"And who are you to tell me I don't belong here?"

He looked very tired, suddenly. "You'll burn out, you'll get fed up with the place. You'll start hating everything and then you'll leave."

She shrugged. "So? I'm a free person."

"Why ask for the disappointments? The disillusionments? Save yourself the heartache and get out while the going is good."

She stood very still; a sudden spark of suspicion flashed through her mind, then it was gone. "Disappointment and disillusionment are legitimate parts of life, of taking risks and trying new things. I can't live my life afraid of being disappointed or hurt. I don't want a dull, vanilla life. I want chocolate truffles with pecans."

An unexpected smile twitched at the corners of his mouth. "Chocolate truffles with pecans?" he said softly. "Where are you going to find those here?"

She smiled back. "Oh, they're here. If you work hard enough, you can find them."

"And when they're finished?"

"You don't let them get finished. You find more, you make more. That's the trick."

"What if you get tired of chocolate truffles with pecans?"

"I've never known anybody who got tired of chocolate truffles with pecans."

His face was expressionless, a mask hiding his thoughts and feelings.

"You know what I'm talking about," she went on. "You're not exactly a vanilla man leading a vanilla life. You've taken a lot of risks yourself to do what you're doing."

His face turned to stone. "And, believe me, I have paid for it." He turned his back on her, as if he'd decided he'd said enough. She watched his back, wondering what had gone through his mind.

"Why ask for the disappointments?" he'd said. So maybe her business wouldn't work out. This, of course, would be a disappointment, but not just for her own sake—in the end that didn't really matter; she could go home and start something else there. The real disappointment would be that she would not have succeeded in helping a few of the people here.

She looked at Ross's back, which was rigid with tension, as were his neck and shoulders. She wondered what he'd really meant, what it was he wasn't telling her, and the answer was there, somewhere very close to the surface, but she couldn't quite grasp it. She longed to go up to him and massage the tension out of him.

"I'm not leaving," she said quietly. "I'm prepared to take the risks."

He turned, almost violently. "Well, I'm not!" he said harshly, his eyes blazing. He grasped her shoulders and looked straight into her eyes, and there was something terrible there—pain and fear such as she had not seen before.

"You're not what?" she whispered.

"I'm not prepared to take the risks!"

She felt her legs begin to shake, and the answer to her question was suddenly clear, very clear. She swallowed, her lips moving, but no words came.

And then he was kissing her. It was not a gentle kiss. It was hard and desperate and hungry. For a moment she was stunned, standing in his arms without moving.

He stopped kissing her suddenly, still holding her tight against him. She heard his ragged breathing, heard her own wild heartbeat. Her legs were shaking, and when he finally let go of her, she almost lost her balance. She sagged into the nearest chair.

"It's so easy for you, isn't it?" he said. "Happy-go-lucky, always laughing, having fun. Everybody loves you. And then the fun is over and you leave. When the rains come, or maybe at the end of the year when the harmattan arrives. Everything choking with sand and dust, and suddenly the fun and excitement are gone and you'll leave. You'll pack your bags, disgusted, because you hate the place. Because things don't work the way you want them to and everything is dirty and you can't stand not having a decent meal once in a while or a shopping spree at Saks or Bloomingdale's and you're bored out of your skull and there's no TV and you can't understand why I bury myself in this place because nothing is going to change in another hundred years and why waste my time?" His voice was hard and furious.

"Stop it!" she cried out. "Ross, stop it!"

All the life seemed to drain out of his face. His eyes were empty, his face expressionless. He raked his hands through his hair and turned his back on her again.

"Go," he said tonelessly. "Just leave. Leave me alone."

She stared at him, shaking, feeling a mingling of fear and fury, and also compassion. A terrible pain raged inside him and had made him lose control.

One part of her was indignantly demanding an apology. Another part of her said to leave him alone and go home. That was what she did when she found her legs steady enough to move.

She knew, she finally knew. His wife had left him because she didn't like living in Obalabi. All the angry predictions he'd hurled at her had simply been the things that had happened to his wife. She'd got bored living in Obalabi and she had left him.

Now Ross didn't want to fall in love with her because she would leave too. So he wanted her to leave before it was too late. It was simple, so simple.

"Does Ross or anyone else ever talk about his wife?" she asked Vicky the following night over rice and mutton stew.

Vicky shook her head. "I've never heard him say anything. Nora made a comment once, something about his wife always being bored. She was always complaining that there was nothing to do." Vicky's mouth turned down.

"I sense no great sympathy here," Sasha commented.

Vicky shrugged. "Maybe it's not fair to judge. I mean, this was years ago and I never even met her, but how can you say there is nothing to do? There is so much to do here, it boggles the mind. Look at you. You figured out something to do within a few weeks!" She picked up the platter of sliced pineapple and paw paw and slid some fruit onto her plate. "Here, you want some?"

Sasha helped herself to some fruit and digested Vicky's words.

"It's Ross's birthday next Sunday," Vicky went on, the subject of Ross's ex-wife apparently forgotten. "Let's plan a party and invite everyone. Nora usually plans the parties, but I told her I'd love to help out." The Branscoms had come back from home leave a couple of weeks ago, refreshed and loaded down with new clothes, yoghurt culture, instant mashed potatoes and assorted other goodies.

"We'll have the party at their house," Vicky went on. "It's bigger, and Daniella and Marc will be here that weekend too. Maybe we can dance."

Ross's birthday. A party. Dancing. Sasha saw possibilities here. She couldn't just give up on him, could she? She couldn't allow herself to accept a situation that was intolerable. She would simply have to prove to him that she could keep herself entertained. That she wasn't going to run because she wanted a shopping spree at Bloomingdale's. That she would not panic when her nail polish ran out.

Somehow she would have to show him her feelings were real. She would have to find herself in a situation with him when his guard was down, when he would let go of that mask of cool composure, when he would show himself to her. Three times he had kissed her. Three times she had seen the mask come down. He wanted her and she wanted him.

Party. Dancing. She could feel his arms around her, feel the warmth of his mouth. Images formed in her head—Ross kissing her, Ross making love to her, tenderly, passionately. She wanted so much to make love to him. Maybe after the party... She took a deep breath.

"So, let's plan," she said to Vicky.

They planned, and Vicky and Sasha traveled to Ouagadougou and raided the shops full of luscious foods from France. They spent the night at L'Hôtel de l'Independance, Sasha's treat, and swam in the pool and had a decadent French dinner and thoroughly enjoyed the luxury of their surroundings.

"A mini vacation," Vicky was saying. "Now and then a necessity to keep everything in perspective."

The next day, while Vicky was at the hospital, Sasha was in the kitchen cooking and baking with the help of fun-loving Saamo, who was enjoying the anticipation and loved trying out the unfamiliar foods. Canned peaches passed, green olives did not.

Daniella and Marc Penbrooke arrived early Sunday morning and settled themselves in the Branscoms' house, which had been decorated with streamers and balloons. It made them feel very welcome, they said, even though the decorations weren't meant for them.

The Penbrookes were passing through on their way to Timbuktu. "Going to see the big bad desert tamed," Daniella said to Sasha over lunch. "A little piece of it at any rate."

Marc told them about the huge irrigation project they were going to visit and the fantastic produce being cultivated.

"I can't wait to see Timbuktu," said Daniella, spearing a piece of pineapple on her fork. "Camels wandering through the streets, they tell me."

Sasha was intrigued. Timbuktu had always seemed like a make-believe place, but of course it was not. It was a very real desert town and right there on the map. She envied them their trip.

"Let me know how it is," she said. "Maybe I'll take a trip up there one day."

Daniella laughed. "I'm surprised to find you're still here. I thought you'd be long gone."

"I like it here. Vicky invited me to stay and I've started a small business and I'd like to see if I can make it work."

After lunch she showed Daniella some of the clothes waiting to be shipped to Accra. Daniella loved them. She shook her head, and began to laugh. "I can't help but think about the way Ross described you—an old maiden aunt who worked in a second-hand clothing store. And here you are, gorgeous and smart and back in business. He must be having the surprise of his life."

"He doesn't want me here," Sasha said, the words coming out without conscious thought. "He can't wait to see me gone."

Daniella stared at her, blue eyes big and surprised. "What makes you think that? Why does he want you gone?"

Sasha swallowed hard. "He doesn't want to be involved."

Daniella bit her lip and gave her a thoughtful look. "And he's afraid he will be."

"Yes."

"He's probably expecting that what happened once will happen again."

Sasha clenched her hands. "I'm not his wife! Dammit, I resent that he treats me as if I'm like her, as if I'll do what she did! I don't even *know* her!"

Daniella gave her a searching look. "You love him, don't you?" she asked softly.

Sasha sighed. "How stupid can I get?"

"Stupid has nothing to do with it. And for what it's worth, you've got a whole lot more guts than Angela will ever have. And you're at least as beautiful, as well dressed, and . . ." Daniella stopped, giving a half smile.

"And what?"

Daniella took her hand. "And your nails are at least as gorgeous as hers."

"Well, that's a relief," said Sasha derisively.

Daniella's face sobered. "I'm sorry, I didn't mean to make a joke out of it, but Angela had this thing about nails. It drove everybody crazy."

"Well, I don't have a thing about nails. I'll cut them and take the polish off if that's what bothers him."

Daniella shook her head. "The problem isn't you. The problem is him. Be patient. He's a smart man. Maybe he'll see the folly of his ways and come around."

"Did you know his wife very well?"

Daniella shook her head. "I only knew her briefly. She left shortly after we came to Ghana. I once spent an entire afternoon listening to her many grievances. She'd had it with territories primitive. They'd lived in New Guinea for a number of years. As I understand it, they had a small plane and a landing strip so she could get out. She made regular jaunts to Hong

Kong and Sydney for regenerative doses of modern civilization. It got a little more difficult living in Obalabi. Getting to the airport isn't so easy, as we all know. One day she packed up and never came back."

"I'm sure he did not take that well."

Daniella shook her head. "Not well."

When Ross arrived for dinner that evening, he looked genuinely startled at the lavish decorations. "Good God," he said, "I don't believe this."

They all laughed, then broke out in singing "Happy Birthday." Dinner was a big success. They all ate like starved wolves of the delicious food—a variety of hors d'oeuvres, barbecued steaks, baked potatoes with sour cream, salad with Roquefort dressing and a cheesecake birthday cake for dessert.

"Sasha did it," Vicky said.

Ross raised a surprised brow. "Don't I remember you saying something about not cooking?" he asked.

She gave a wicked smile. "I lied."

Over coffee, Ross opened his gifts. Paperback books, a bottle of whiskey, fresh apples, a T-shirt. Sasha had found the present she wanted: a box of chocolate truffles with nuts. She watched with a thumping heart as he unwrapped her gift. He looked at it for a long moment, reading the note she'd taped to the box.

If you really want chocolate truffles with pecans, you can find them, even here.

He looked up, met her eyes and gave a funny little smile. "Thank you," he said. "Look at this, folks, a real decadent gift, this one."

"Chocolates?" Daniella whispered in Sasha's ear, obviously surprised.

"I tried to be original, decadent and frivolous," Sasha whispered back. "The man needs a little frivolity."

Daniella chuckled. "I think you may be right. The man is altogether too sober. I'm glad someone's trying to lighten him up."

Vicky had gathered, from the various guests, a very eclectic assortment of dance music—country songs, tunes from the sixties, and even reggae. She put on some reggae and she and Jochen started dancing in the living room, which had been cleared of furniture. Several others followed suit.

Sasha glanced across the veranda where Ross was talking to Marc Penbrooke. She saw Daniella come and drag her husband off to dance. Ross stood up and looked around, meeting her eyes. She watched him come toward her, feeling her pulse leap, feeling again the aching need inside her.

"Care to dance?" he asked.

She said she did.

"Thank you for a great dinner," he said as they moved to the dance floor. "Getting all that must not have been easy."

"You only have a birthday once a year," she said lightly. "And since I happened to know what your favorite meal is, how could I resist?"

He gave a crooked smile. "And the chocolates. Quite a find."

She met his eyes and warmth suffused her. "If you really want something," she said, feeling oddly shaky, "you do what it takes." She smiled then, in an attempt to make her remark a casual one, but of course it was not, and of course he knew it.

Like the rest of them, they danced without touching. "When was the last time you danced?" she asked, swaying to the music.

He shrugged. "I don't remember. No, not true, I do remember. Last year, actually. On St. Barlow, a small island in the Caribbean."

"On an island in the Caribbean? What were you doing there?"

"I was on home leave, visiting the Penbrookes. They spend a month there every year. Marc's father owns a house on the beach there, and GHO built a small teaching hospital on the island and I wanted to see it. Anyway, there was a big party and we danced."

"Thousands of islands, and GHO builds a teaching hospital on the same one that the Penbrookes have a house?"

"Oh, it's no coincidence. Marc's father is a wealthy businessman and he and Bucks are big buddies."

"Who's Bucks?"

"The old goat who runs GHO."

She nodded. "The eccentric billionaire with a vision."

"Right."

"Do you like the Caribbean?"

He said he did. The climate was wonderful. St. Barlow was beautiful. There were plenty of recreational opportunities—fishing, sailing, swimming, snorkeling and scuba diving. It all sounded quite idyllic. Had she ever been to the Caribbean? he asked, and she said no, but she'd spent a couple of months trekking through rural Mexico. Her other travels had been to Canada and Europe, which had been experiences of a less primitive nature.

A slow dance followed and she was in his arms. Exactly where she wanted to be. It had been inevitable, of course. And it felt right to be there, as natural as the sun and the rain. The song was a schmaltzy German love song. Although she did not understand the words, it took no imagination to know what they meant. If there was any doubt at all, looking at Vicky and Jochen would clear things up. They looked transported.

Sasha was beginning to feel transported herself. She felt Ross's body move against hers, his warmth coming through her clothes, touching her skin. Her nerves tingled. Her blood sang. Need flooded every cell of her being. She wanted to melt into him, hide against the strong wall of his chest.

He relaxed his grip on her right hand and dropped it on his shoulder, moving her even closer against him. She slipped both arms around his neck and she felt his cheek against hers. She closed her eyes, and she no longer felt the floor beneath her feet. She was floating.

The song went on and on. Or maybe it was another song already, equally schmaltzy, she wasn't sure.

She wanted to be alone with him. She wanted to kiss him and tell him how she felt. She wanted to be together in some quiet place where they could share their true feelings with each other—no masks, no pretense. She wanted . . . Involuntarily she moved closer against him. He wanted her too. His cool control had melted away and his body molded itself against her. They moved as in a dream.

He stopped dancing in the middle of the song. He caught her hand and without a word led her out of the open doors into the shadowed garden. The crickets chirped enthusiastically. There was the sweet scent of some night-flowering bloom, and stars festooned the velvet sky. There was no time to contemplate the magic of the night. Under the canopy of a twisted tree, he drew her up against him and the world fell away. He kissed her fiercely and a storm of yearning unleashed itself inside her. There was madness in the night. His mouth and hands created magic and her body was alive with sensation.

She could not see him. The moon was hidden and the dark seemed filled with a pagan power, its force sweeping them away from thought and sanity. She was trembling in his embrace, breathless, transfixed. He drew away suddenly, breathing raggedly, and once more took her hand, leading her away without a word. She followed as if in a trance, not seeing where they were going until they were in front of Ross's house and he was pushing open the door. It swung closed behind them. He steered her through the living room into his bedroom and he pulled her back into his arms, his hands on her hips, drawing her close against him. She leaned into him, unresisting, and his mouth closed over hers with bruising intensity. His kiss was like a fire that seared her body and soul. Then he was taking off her clothes, touching her body, and she thought she was going mad. He tore off his own clothes and held her again, close and desperate and then, finally, through all the hot wildness, a flicker of fear began to lick at her mind. There was no gentleness, no love in the heat of his passion. He seemed like a man possessed.

"Ross!" she whispered fiercely. She pushed at his chest with all her might. "Ross!"

"This is what you wanted, isn't it?" he said roughly. "This is what you wanted all night!"

"No!" she said, and she was suddenly appalled at what was happening.

"No?" He gave a mocking laugh.

"No!" she said. "Not like this, I didn't!" She began to tremble violently. "You're *angry* and you're taking it out on me." Her voice shook. "No, that's not how I want it! Spare me your caveman heroics!"

He stared at her, and the fury and the passion drained out of his face, as if some demon had suddenly lost its grip on him. He dropped himself on the bed and threw his arm across his face. "Oh, my God," he said, his voice tortured.

"I thought you wanted to make love to me," she said, feeling tears come to her eyes. "Why are you so angry? What did I do?"

"You did nothing." He jerked himself upright. "I don't want to want you, dammit!" he said, and the anger was back in his voice, tinged with undeniable desperation.

She stood there like a fool, naked, with tears running down her face. He didn't want to want her.

But he did. And it made him furious. She grabbed her clothes off the floor. She was leaving. No way was she staying where she wasn't wanted.

He gave a muffled curse and leaped off the bed, dragging her back with him, holding her naked body close to his. "Don't cry, please don't cry." He was stroking her hair. "I'm sorry. God, I'm such a bastard."

She struggled against him. "Let go of me!" Her voice was thick and new tears streamed down her cheeks. "Let go of me!"

"No," he said, "I'm not letting you go."

She lay rigidly in his arms, hating him, hating her own weakness. There was no strength in her to fight him. His body was braced above hers, powerful, darkly tanned, supremely male. Despite her anger she could feel herself respond, an insidious, treacherous warmth creeping through her, softening, melting. Her hands, clenched into fists, began to relax. She felt the soothing touch of his hand on her hair, his mouth kissing her wet eyes. All wildness had left him and his embrace was full of exquisite, tender caring. It was what she had wanted: the loving, the gentleness that was so much a part of him.

"I'm sorry," he whispered. "I'm sorry I was such a bastard."

She lay with her eyes closed, saying nothing, feeling her anger melting away.

"I've ached to hold you," he said huskily, his lips stroking hers with intoxicating sensuality. His breath was warm on her mouth and her lips parted instinctively. She could no longer lie still. She yearned to touch him, love him, show him the depth of her feelings. Her arms slipped around him, drawing him closer to her. He turned her slightly, to take some of his weight off. His mouth took hers, kissing her deeply, and she responded, sweet longing sweeping through her.

Then his hold on her relaxed slightly. He raised his head, looking into her eyes with a sweet, loving passion. One hand caressed her right breast. "You're beautiful and soft and warm," he said softly. "You feel so good here in my bed."

His words were like champagne, tingling through her blood. Her heart flowed over with love. She curled her fingers into the thick, soft hair, smiling in response. He went on stroking her breast.

"I want to make love to you—with you."

"Yes," she said, knowing he needed to hear her say it.

He leaned closer again, his mouth trailing a path across her cheek to her ear. "This isn't very romantic," he whispered then, "but we need to do something about contraceptives."

She smiled against his cheek, feeling sudden humor tickling her throat. "I already did," she whispered back. "I helped myself to some free samples from the clinic this morning."

"This morning?"

She put her face against the warmth of his neck. "Yes." She swallowed. "I was thinking of the party, of you and me. I've wanted to make love with you so much, Ross, and I was hoping . . . anyway, I didn't want to be stupid about it."

He chuckled. "You are a devious woman," he said.

He lifted his face and looked into her eyes with humor. She felt her face grow warm. I'm thirty years old, she thought, and I'm blushing like a teenager. It's embarrassing. She lifted her chin.

"So I gave myself away," she said.

He chuckled and brushed his lips over her temple. "It wasn't any big secret, was it? I've wanted you, too, for quite some time." His arms tightened around her. "Let me show you how much."

It started with a sensuous brush of his mouth, the gentle touch of his hands in her hair, cradling her head. His tongue stroked her lips, taking its time before venturing inside, finding hers, starting a seductive little dance. His mouth was warm and insistent, taking command, and she savored the sensation. She lay breathlessly beneath him, feeling, for the moment, so bewitched that all she could do was lie there and let him make magic.

And he did.

His hands played her body like a delicate instrument. With every caress and every kiss, he made her tremble more, made her senses soar higher and higher. Her body sang to his touch.

"You know what you've done to me, don't you?" he said softly, raising his head to look into her eyes. Moonlight spilled into the room, but his face above her was in shadow.

She shook her head. "No."

He stroked her hair. "You with your red hair and green eyes. You've been driving me crazy." His voice was husky, unsteady. "You've invaded my dreams, you've crawled under my skin."

His mouth found her breast and she could not help the soft moan of pure pleasure. His tongue played an erotic little game with her nipple, sucking, stroking, sending tingling sensations all through her, setting her on fire.

She could no longer lie still. She needed to move against him, touch him, stroke his body, which felt hot to the touch. She wanted to taste him. So her hands and mouth moved, stroking, searching, delighting in his powerful male body—the strength of muscle, the heat of his skin, the crispness of the hair on his chest. She reveled in the taste of him, the clean, male scent of him. He wanted her. And she wanted him. It was a glorious feeling to be able, finally, to give in to it—to still the painful yearning she felt for him, to express herself with him in this most intimate of ways, so show him truly how she felt.

"You make me feel so good," she whispered. "I've never felt like this before." It was true. This all-consuming, joyous desire was not like anything she had experienced before.

A soft groan came from deep inside him and for a moment he lay still against her, breathing heavily. Then he moved again, his lovemaking more passionate now, the restraint gone. She gave him back kind for kind, relishing the feel of his strong body under her hands, the beating of his heart against her cheek, the sound of his breathing.

"I need you," he muttered. "Oh, God, how I want you."

The words were like music, filling her heart. "I need you too," she whispered. And she did. She needed him not just tonight, but always. Crazy, crazy, she thought incoherently. Love is crazy. Love is wonderful. His hand moved up the inside of her thigh, finding the warm, secret places there, tantalizing her beyond endurance. She felt her body grow liquid and weightless, and she knew the fire inside her was out of control and could no longer be contained. "Please," she whispered against his mouth. "I want to feel you inside me."

He moved over her, his mouth hot on hers, and then he was inside her and it was better than anything she had dared dream, the warm, intoxicating sensation of their bodies entwined, moving together in a delirious dance of desire.

It was a tumultuous, wondrous loving, and the fire was sweet and hot until it was extinguished in a final flare of brilliant light.

They lay silently in each other's arms. She was flushed and breathless, feeling rich and utterly fulfilled. She smiled to herself, snuggling closer in his embrace, amazed at how perfectly they fitted together.

The morning light was hard and bright, and she awoke alone in Ross's bed, hearing the squawking of the chickens and the hard sound of a woman's angry voice coming from the mud-hut compound.

She lay very still, remembering last night, listening to the silence of the house, feeling apprehension creep through her bones. Something wasn't right.

She looked for her clothes. Her skirt lay crumpled at the foot of the bed, and the rest of her clothes had slipped on to the floor. She dragged them on, feeling in the grip of some odd fear. The house seemed empty and silent, but she found Ross on the veranda with a cup of coffee.

"Good morning," he said evenly. After a night of passionate loving his tone was heartrendingly formal. She wanted to go to him and be enfolded in a warm and intimate embrace but, looking at his remote face, she knew with bitter certainty that an embrace, intimate or otherwise, was not forthcoming. There was no sweetness left; it had dissolved in the harsh morning light. The love and tenderness of the night had vanished with the stars.

"Ross?" she said softly. It was a question, a plea.

"Would you like a cup of coffee?" he asked. "There's a fresh pot."

"No, thank you." Her throat ached. Whatever he had been contemplating, sitting here on the veranda in the early-morning light, it had not been the beginning of a meaningful relationship.

"What's wrong?" she asked.

He lifted a quizzical brow. "Wrong? Nothing."

"I don't understand you," she said, feeling a choking sensation.

"What don't you understand?"

"Oh, don't act like that! We've spent hours making love to each other and now you treat me as if I'm some stranger off the street."

"I'm sorry," he said evenly, and drained his coffee.

She felt a flash of fury. "Sorry for what?"

He put his cup down and pushed his hands into his pockets. "For hurting you. I'm not denying there are feelings and emotions between us. I just want you to realize this won't lead to anything." He talked in a sober, analytical voice, the voice of a scientist explaining an experiment.

"Oh, I see," she said derisively.

"I don't want to give you the wrong impression, Sasha."

"How gracious of you," she said bitterly. "And what wrong impression would that be?" She felt wounded to the depths of her soul. She wanted to cry. She wanted to hit him.

He rubbed the back of his neck. "The impression that we have initiated a more...intimate relationship. I don't want to hurt you, but I thought it would be fair to let you know."

"Oh, and I should thank you for your honesty, no doubt. God, you are a swine, Ross."

He flinched at her words. "It has nothing to do with you," he said tonelessly. "It has something to do with me. I don't want...I prefer not to...get involved."

She felt her heart grow stone-cold. "So where does last night fit in?"

"We wanted each other."

Right, she thought. That was about the gist of it. Grow up, honey, she told herself. People sleep with each other for want of better reasons all the time. "A one-night stand, then," she said caustically. "How lovely. Of course it won't happen again."

He was silent, his face inscrutable.

How can you possibly think, she asked him silently, that it won't happen again? How can you look at me and not know the truth? How dare you cheapen what happened between us?

"We wanted each other." How cold, how calculating it sounded. Yet that was not how it had been. Behind that impenetrable mask with which he presented her now, there was another side of him—a deeply passionate, generous, loving side. He had given her that part of himself last night. He hadn't made love to her as if she were merely a conveniently available female.

He had made love to her as if he loved her. No one could be that much of an actor. She felt a deep sorrow overwhelm her and she fought the urge to burst into tears.

"I'm sorry you feel the way you do," she said with difficulty. She straightened her shoulders, collected her dignity and walked out of the house.

All she kept hearing in her head were his words: "I don't want to want you, dammit."

She went to the under-fives clinic at nine, bringing with her a couple of brand-new nutrition posters she had painted in bright colors.

Vicky and her student assistant were already there. The posters were much admired and hung up.

"Ross was in a foul mood this morning," Vicky informed her as they stepped back to have another look at the posters. "What do you suppose happened last night? He liked the party, didn't he?"

Sasha's mouth opened and closed. Vicky, obviously, had not realized that she hadn't come home last night. And when she hadn't shown up for breakfast this morning Vicky had probably assumed she was sleeping in after the party.

"I don't know," Sasha lied. The lie was bitter in her mouth. She knew very well why Ross was in a foul mood. He'd had second thoughts about last night.

She heard the crying of a child as she walked along the breezeway back to the exit. It was coming from one of the small treatment rooms whose door was half-open. Automatically she glanced inside and there was Ross in his white coat, holding a small boy in his lap, the mother hovering anxiously by his side.

She stopped, transfixed, as she watched Ross gently soothing the child. She couldn't see what was wrong with the little boy—there were no outward signs of injury. Vaguely she heard Ross's voice, speaking in the tribal language, his tone soft and reassuring. The child began to calm down, and Ross was smiling now, his face warm and caring.

She felt a lump in her throat and she stood rooted to the ground, staring at his face. Everything began to swim before her eyes and she forced her legs to move and carry her away.

The days passed in a blur of misery. His behavior toward her was aloof and distant. She wished she knew how to puncture the hard shell of his indifference.

"*I don't want to want you.*" The words were like shards of glass lodged in her chest and she kept wavering between anger and pain. She needed advice, but there wasn't anyone to give it. No friendly clergyman, no therapist, no friend close enough. She wished there were a bookstore with self-help books. *What to Do with a Man who Doesn't Want to Want You but Does.*

First of all, she needed an honest answer to the question if she wanted to be wanted by the man who didn't want to want her.

The answer was yes.

Then perhaps the question that ought to follow was, Why did he not want to want her? And she already knew the answer to that: he had no intention of suffering through a repeat performance of his failed marital relationship.

He was taking it for granted that she was going to leave, eventually. Making an investment in a relationship was asking for trouble. How could she possibly convince him she wasn't going to run out on him?

She groaned. Her head ached. All this thinking was bad for her health. This whole situation wasn't doing her much good. Unrequited love could make people sick. She frowned at the thought. There was an idea in there somewhere. Maybe she would get sick. She'd end up in the hospital and he would be her doctor, unable to cure her with any traditional medical methods. The only way to cure her was for him to give her the magic of his love.

She groaned. She was going nuts already.

* * *

Sasha was sitting in the living room reading that night when a sound attracted her attention—the rumbling of a truck coming down the road. She frowned and looked at her watch. At this hour? It was almost ten. At ten, the town was asleep, except for the people in the Don't Mind Your Wife Bar.

She got up and looked out of the window, seeing the *tro tro* stop in front of the house. Who could it be? Someone was climbing out, a man, but it was very dark and she didn't recognize him. Opening the door, she switched on the outside light and the man who'd just arrived was flooded with light.

She felt her mouth fall open and she snapped her jaws together. "*Richard*?" she asked incredulously. "Is that you?"

CHAPTER SEVEN

"WHAT'S left of me," Richard said sourly.

Sasha couldn't help staring at him. It couldn't be true. It was impossible. She could not believe the man in front of her was Richard. She hardly recognized him. He was dusty, sweaty, his hair dull and disheveled—all the polish and shine of his normally immaculate yuppie exterior annihilated by this alien environment. Richard was never sweaty. Richard's hair was never disheveled.

She laughed. She couldn't help it. "Oh, Richard, I can't believe this is you!" It wasn't until then that she realized there was someone else behind him, another man. He was old, bald-headed but for a thick, white, curly fringe around the lower edges of his scalp. He was skinny and straight as an arrow. He wore enormous, baggy tartan shorts, a red T-shirt and dusty Nikes that looked like boats on the end of his skinny white legs. He looked like a caricature.

"I'm sorry, I didn't see you," she said.

The man laughed, his sharp dark eyes observing her keenly. "You didn't miss much." He slapped Richard on the shoulder. "If you're all right now, son, I'll go find a bed of my own and give these old bones a rest." He turned and loped down the path.

She stared after him in amazement. Where was he going to find a bed? she wondered. The *tro tro* had left. It was night.

"Where is he going?"

"How do I know?" Richard snapped, stepping inside. "The man is a nutcase, escaped from the loony bin. He says he owns the hospital. He belongs in one."

Sasha watched the man turn into Ross's drive. He pounded on the front door. "Ross!" he boomed. "Let me in!"

She grinned and closed the door. Ross was having a visitor too.

Richard dragged his suitcase farther into the room and collapsed on the couch, throwing his head back and letting out a deep sigh. "Good God, I was afraid I would never find you."

"Well, you did, but why you wanted to is a mystery to me."

He opened his eyes and looked at her. "I don't suppose I'm fit to be kissed," he said.

"You're perfectly fit to be kissed, only I'm not going to." Dust and dirt was not what held her back. Richard was history. It had been difficult for him to accept, she knew. How difficult was only now clear. Richard only traveled first class. Richard only slept in top-notch hotels with room service.

And now Richard had braved the wilds of Africa to come to see her. He must be desperate. Very, very desperate, going by the total ruin of him. Sprawled on the couch, he looked limp and dehydrated. She went into the kitchen and brought him a glass of iced tea to revive him.

He took it gratefully and gulped it down. "I cannot believe this place," he said almost breathlessly. "I did not think I would survive the day."

"How did you get here?"

"I flew in to Tamale, or whatever that name of that miserable little town is, on some ancient propeller plane. Bucks was on it too."

"Bucks?" Where had she heard that name before? Of course! Ross had mentioned him. Bucks was the eccentric billionaire with a vision who ran GHO. The man she had just seen outside did not look like any billionaire she had ever seen. Just thinking of the excruciatingly ugly shorts and his skinny legs made her want to laugh.

"The nutcase," Richard explained. "Buckley, I think his name is, but everybody calls him Bucks, or so he says. Anyway, I couldn't find transportation to come here. There were no more planes. I could not rent a car. The bus had left. Then Bucks came up to me and asked where I was going. That's when he told me he was going to the same place and got us on that decrepit truck. For hours on end I sat there squashed between two enormous women breast-feeding their squalling infants. It was appalling. There was somebody with a damned *pig* on board, smelling up the place. I must reek to high heaven."

"Don't worry," she said, trying desperately not to laugh. "Nobody minds."

"You think this is funny?" he asked.

"It is funny, Richard. Very funny. Now tell me why you're here."

"You must know why. I'm worried about you." He struggled to straighten his wilted limbs, arranging his features in an expression of indulgent solicitude in an obvious attempt to reconstruct his collapsed composure. "In fact, I am quite concerned."

"Oh? I don't understand."

"I was waiting for you to come back, and you didn't, and——"

"Why were you waiting? You know I had no intention of coming back to you. Our relationship was a mistake. My mistake—I take full responsibility, but it's finished."

"I understand how you feel. I realize I said some things that were not . . . very flattering and——"

The understatement of the year. "You can say that again."

His expression grew more solemn. "You must understand I was under considerable stress when you broke off our relationship, and very hurt."

"I understand." She had no desire to argue with him. "But whatever you are hoping to gain here is not going to happen, Richard." She felt anger begin to build. He had come here without an invitation, without even telling her he was on the way. She didn't want him here. She was ready to give him the full treatment verbally, but seeing his exhausted face she decided to have mercy on him, temporarily at least. Tomorrow was another day.

"I need something to eat," he stated. "I'm starving. All I had all day was some bananas and peanuts. God knows what the stuff was they were concocting in those pots by the road."

"I'll see what there is." She rose to her feet. The refrigerator yielded little, only a small amount of millet and guinea-fowl stew. Well, if he was hungry, he'd eat it. She heated it up, put it on a plate and carried it into the living room.

He was still sitting in the same slumped position. "Here you go," she said, handing him the plate.

He looked at it suspiciously. "What is this stuff?"

"Food," she snapped. "We're a little short on Brie and smoked salmon here."

He made no further comment and began to eat.

"You're putting me in quite a spot," she said. "I had no idea you were coming, and I have no bed for you."

"No bed?" He looked appalled. "I travel half around the world to see you and you have no bed for me? I am exhausted, jet-lagged. I need sleep."

"You may not have noticed but this is not the Hilton. This is a very small bungalow. There are two bedrooms. Vicky has one. I have the other. There's a single bed in each of them and that's the extent of the beds in this house. You may have the couch, and tomorrow I'll have someone take you to the Rest In Peace Rest House."

He gulped and his eyes popped out. "The what?"

She bit her lip, trying not to laugh. "The Rest In Peace Rest House. I didn't name it, so don't blame me. They have beds there, very cheap too. If you're lucky, the generator works and there's electricity, but don't count on it."

He jerked himself upright. "Listen," he began, furious, "this is——"

Her body grew rigid. "No! You listen to me! Keep your voice down! Vicky is sleeping and she needs her rest. If you don't shut up you can sleep outside with the mosquitoes and snakes!"

He rubbed his eyes, sagging back against the couch cushions. "All right, all right."

Later, as she lay in bed, Sasha contemplated the situation, and it wasn't altogether funny. Oh, damn! she thought. What am I going to do with him? She needed another self-help book: What to Do with a

Man who Wants You but You Don't Want Him to Want You.

In the morning Ross stopped by to see Vicky. They were sitting in the living room with their coffee, having just finished breakfast.

"Bucks is here," he announced. "If you see a skinny bald-headed guy wandering around the hospital in baggy shorts, it's him."

Vicky's eyes lit up. "I didn't know he was coming," she said.

"You never know when he's coming. He just drops in. He pounded on my door last night at ten. That's usually how I know he's here."

"He came on a *tro tro* last night," Sasha said. "I thought billionaires had private jets."

Ross shrugged. "He has a couple of jets, but sometimes he likes to travel on local transportation. Keeps him in touch with reality, he says." He gave Sasha an amused look. "Don't try to put him in a box. There is no box for him. He defies all descriptions."

Vicky left them to get ready for work as Richard sauntered into the room, a towel wrapped around his waist, an expression of disgust on his face. He had just partaken of his first sip of instant coffee.

"This stuff is vile," he said to Sasha.

"Then, by all means, don't drink it," she said cheerfully. Apart from his scowl, he looked rather manly, his well-exercised body trim and lean. She glanced at Ross, catching, in a fleeting instant, a flash of dark fury in his narrowed eyes. Fury? No, surely she'd misread that. She searched his face more carefully, but there was nothing there. His expression was perfectly bland as he observed Richard.

For a brief moment she considered the possibilities of Richard's sudden appearance. Perhaps it would agitate Ross enough to evaluate his feelings for her. Perhaps, under the pressure of a perceived threat, he might be forced to confront his feelings for her. Jealousy, of course, was a nasty emotion, and not one she would intentionally stir up—she wouldn't sink that low. However, since a perfect situation had presented itself totally without her involvement, she might be forgiven for contemplating the prospects.

Ross jealous. It didn't really seem very feasible, but that was the way it happened in romances. The hero, faced with another male in the running for the heroine's favors, finally realized how much he adored her and, after a manly show of outrage, declared his feelings.

She introduced the two men and held her breath. Richard drew himself up to his full height. He was tall, but not as tall as Ross, and Sasha saw he did not like to be presented with a male who appeared superior in any way. He was showing distinct signs of insecurity, not something that would inspire jealousy. Sasha's hopes, vague as they might have been, evaporated. Ross's face was expressionless.

"Richard is worried about me," she informed Ross, her voice bland. She watched his face. Nothing. He leaned casually against the wall, arms crossed in front of his chest, all calm and relaxed.

Then she noticed his hands and her pulse leaped.

Not so calm and relaxed. His hands, partially hidden by his crossed arms, were balled into fists.

"Sasha's been gone a long time," Richard elaborated. "I was concerned about her, so I thought I'd pop over and see how's she's holding out."

Pop over. Sasha bit her lip. The way he had looked last night, he'd not done any popping. Sweating, swearing and severe suffering would have been a more accurate description. One did not "pop over" to Obalabi.

Ross lifted a skeptical brow. "Concerned?" he echoed.

"I think it's time I took her home," Richard said haughtily, his voice taking on an undeniably proprietorial tone. Sasha gritted her teeth. Then she saw Ross's face and she nearly stopped breathing. He was smiling. Broadly.

"Is that right?" asked Ross.

"Yes," said Richard. "It's high time she forgets all this nonsense and comes home."

"I see," said Ross slowly, still smiling. "I'm afraid you're in for a big disappointment. I think you don't know our Sasha very well."

His comment nearly floored her. For a fraction of a moment she'd thought the smile had been one of delight—delight at seeing her departure as an imminent possibility. *Our* Sasha, he'd said. Suddenly things were not quite as clear as before. One thing that was clear, though, was the fact that Ross was openly amused by the idea of Richard thinking he could take her back home.

Richard was not delighted with Ross's statement. It had hit him right in the gut. His eyes flashed. "I've known her for a lot longer than you have, Doctor!" He tried to stretch another inch out of his spine, which was not a successful endeavor.

Ross pushed himself away from the wall. "Well, there's knowing and there's knowing," he said meaningfully. He inclined his head. "Have a nice stay."

He turned and marched out of the door, leaving Richard fuming with rage.

He faced her, hands on his hips, nostrils flaring. "Are you having an affair with this joker?" he demanded.

"Richard, my personal life is none of your business. Now let's have some breakfast and see if I can find someone with transportation who can take you over to the rest house."

"Is that the best you can do?"

She shrugged. "The best *you* can do, Richard, is to get back on a *tro tro* and go back home. Coming here was sheer insanity, don't you know that?"

His chest expanded slightly. It was a sexy chest with a light mat of dark hair and it didn't do a thing for her. "I think something is seriously wrong with you, Sasha," he said in a funereal voice. He glanced around with distaste at the cluttered room. Boxes of clothes had joined the stacks of books and magazines piled up against the wall. "What sane person would live in a place like this?"

"To tell you the truth, I'm saner now than I've been for a long time."

It was the truth. She felt alive with new energy. She knew what she wanted. She wanted to build a successful business and help people.

And she wanted Ross.

Richard was not having a good time. Sasha eyed him across the table. They were at Christine's house for dinner and of course he had been invited to come along. He didn't know how lucky he was. This afternoon she had transported him to the rest house, where he was now settled in a small room with a fan and a bucket of water in lieu of a shower. He was drinking too much, she noticed. He was also talking too much. He was looking for sympathy for his terrible plight, only no one was feeling sorry for him. They were more interested in listening to Bucks, who was also present, dressed in another pair of baggy shorts and a lurid flowered shirt.

Bucks had stories—witchcraft stories, snake stories and other tales of horror and delight. Every time there was the slightest pause, Richard would offer up another lamentation for public consumption.

Ross was amused. He was watching her. He was watching Richard. He had an insufferable little smirk on his face—not at all the face of a jealous lover. And why would he be jealous, anyway? Richard was making a fool of himself. Ross knew it. She knew it.

Oh, damn, she thought, looking at Ross. Why did it all have to be so complicated? Why couldn't their relationship be simple and straightforward?

She liked simple and straightforward. She was in love with him. She wanted him to be in love with her. She wanted to hold hands and float in the clouds together, delirious, with rose-colored glasses on.

Obviously Ross didn't want any part of this. He wanted no part of her, or at least he was telling himself that he wanted no part of her. It hurt. It hurt to think of the time they had made love. He'd been a different man then, passionate, loving, and he had wanted her.

Feeling angry and despondent, she felt a sudden urge to take her frustrations out on something or somebody. Richard, for instance. If she could have, she would have kicked him under the table.

She got up to go to the kitchen for more iced water, and passed by Richard's chair.

"Richard," she whispered in his ear, "stop the booze, will you? You're making a fool of yourself."

He didn't pay attention to her. After dinner, with even more drink in him, he grabbed her suddenly and pulled her onto his lap.

"All these women today, they're all neurotic, have you noticed? All they want is your money and your body."

"Richard, stop it!" she hissed and wrestled herself off his knees. She caught, in a fleeting instant, Ross's narrowed eyes. Richard's idiotic behavior, so far, had amused him. Richard's touching her did not. Well, it was something.

Richard grinned. "But not my Sasha. She's got her head on straight and she knows what she wants. Here you have one hell of a woman. Doesn't push, doesn't make demands, just goes her own way and has her own life and is happy." He gulped some more whiskey. He glanced importantly around the room and, just as he wanted, he had everybody's undivided attention. Ross, too, was watching the show, his face inscrutable.

"Very talented, very smart," Richard went on. "Believe me, these days it's very important to have an independent woman in your life, one who knows how to take care of herself. Did you know she started her own business? Very impressive. Turned it into a bundle of cash in six years. Don't know why she sold out." His face crumpled like a child about to cry. "Then she said she didn't want me any more." He was getting positively maudlin.

Sasha shook his shoulder. "Stop it, Richard. Have some coffee."

Richard reached for her hand. "I need you in my life, Sasha. Come back with me." Once more he glanced around the room. "I have a very stressful life, you see. It may be hard to understand, living in such a hellhole where nothing happens, but my life is stressful. The zipper industry is extremely competitive. Sasha keeps me in balance, you see. I need her." He closed his eyes and slumped in his chair. "I'm so damned tired," he muttered.

Vicky and Jochen offered to take him back to the RIP Rest House, much to Sasha's relief. It did, however, leave her to ride back home with Ross and Bucks, which was not a relief.

"Well, well," said Ross when they were on the road, Bucks in the back of the Jeep. "That's what you call true, unadulterated love." There was mockery in his voice. "Coming all the way over here, suffering hardship and deprivation to get you back. Very touching."

"It's what you call obsession," commented Bucks. "Ditch the guy, girl. He's a whiner." He grinned at her. "That was quite a list of commendable traits he credited you with. You sound like a woman after my own heart."

"Thank you," she said nicely. What else could she say? "And I did terminate our relationship, but he didn't choose to believe me. He has a rather tenacious possessive streak about him."

"He won't last long here," predicted Bucks. "He'll be gone in a couple of days."

Ross slowed down and turned a corner. "Aren't you a bit cruel letting him stay at the RIP Rest House?"

"Why?" she asked.

"I'd think that was obvious. He doesn't seem the type who's used to taking splash baths with a bucket of water."

"No, he isn't. Maybe he'll learn something. Your concern surprises me, Doc. When you picked me up at the airport you had me sleep my first night in the country on a bunch of boxes in the back of your Jeep. I didn't even have a bucket of water to wash with. I don't recall your having any sympathy for me whatsoever."

His mouth curved into a smile. "You're not the type to go looking for sympathy, are you?"

"No. It's not one of the emotions I aspire to elicit in people."

"What do you like people to feel toward you?"

"Awe's good," she said, deadpan. "Blind admiration for my accomplishments. Deep respect for my intellect." She shrugged. "I don't worry a whole lot about what people think about me."

"Excellent," said Bucks in the back. "As I said, a woman after my own heart. Ross, my boy, why don't you try your luck? I'm a bit too ripe for her, or I'd give it a try myself."

"You're only seventy-nine," Ross said dryly. "With all your money, that's young."

Bucks chuckled. "So that's why. I keep wondering what all these young things see in a bald-headed old coot like me."

"It isn't your legs, Bucks."

Bucks roared.

They drove on through the cool, dark night, past the deserted market and the Don't Mind Your Wife Bar. Music spilled out into the night.

"Let me off here," ordered Bucks. "I'm feeling the urge to do a little socio-anthropological research."

Without comment, Ross brought the Jeep to a stop and got out to give Bucks the chance to extricate his long-limbed body, which he did with amazing agility.

"Does the man not get tired?" Sasha asked as they drove on.

"He doesn't believe in being tired. Sleep is a waste of time, according to him."

"How is he going to come home? It's late."

"He always finds a way. Besides, it's only two miles or so. He'll probably walk. And sing."

"Sing?"

"He always sings when he walks."

Sasha laughed. "Are you sure he is seventy-nine?"

Ross nodded. "He'll live to be one hundred and twenty, if not older."

She wouldn't be surprised.

She was glad to have a topic of discussion. She felt awkward being alone with Ross. Ever since the night they had made love, the tension between them had become excruciating, like a live thing between them. She was relieved when they were home.

Even with the distraction of Richard's annoying presence, Ross stayed on her mind the following days. She kept remembering their night of loving in vivid detail. Indelibly printed in her mind were Ross's tender touches, his sensuous kisses, his smoldering eyes. He'd been a different man then. She wanted that man.

The need to have him look at her, touch her, the need to hear his voice was becoming overwhelming. She felt in the grip of some crazy, unfocused nightmare. There was Richard, begging for her eternal devotion, which she could not bestow on him; there was Ross, avoiding her like the plague while her heart leaped in her chest every time she managed to catch a glimpse of him; there was Bucks in his atrocious shorts advising Ross to focus romantic attention on her because she was a jewel among women, so Bucks said.

Richard, after several days of hectic pursuit, came to the fortunate conclusion that his mission was an ill-fated one. If Sasha wanted to ruin her life, then so be it. He could no longer hang around and wait for her to come to her senses. The zipper business would perish if he didn't return soon. The life-style in Obalabi did not agree with his mind or his body. He was not resting in peace at the Rest In Peace Rest House. There were cockroaches, he said. And lizards on the ceiling and a bonanza of other exotic creatures unknown to science. Food, too, was a problem. He wanted salmon, and a good steak. He would settle for a humble hamburger. There was no hamburger to settle for, humble or otherwise. During the night, as he held vigil to ward off the creepy crawlies, he hallucinated about food. He described in mouth-watering detail the choice edibles he saw floating around the squalid room. Scottish smoked salmon, pâté de foie gras, sautéd trout, wine in Waterford crystal, chocolate mousse.

The chocolate mousse almost did her in. "Shut up," she said. "You're making me sick."

He was using up, with frightening speed, her normally large reservoir of patience.

"What does it take to get a cup of espresso here?" he wailed on the third day of his sojourn.

"A miracle," said Sasha, pitiless.

This did it.

"I'm going home," he announced, and packed his bag.

Bucks was also packing his bag, having satisfied himself that the hospital was doing what it was supposed to be doing. He was taking off to Brazil where in the Amazon interior a new hospital was being put into operation. Bucks managed to escape in Joe's chauffeur-driven Mercedes-Benz before Richard could prevail upon him to give him a ride.

"I think," he'd said to Ross as he was saying goodbye, "that you ought to work on her." He'd nodded in Sasha's direction. "Not many of her kind around, and believe me I've been around."

Her heart bolted into her throat at his words. Ross glowered at Bucks. "Mind your own business," he said and Bucks laughed, not at all put out. Bucks simply was not to be put out.

"Ross, my boy, I think it's about time you got over that useless female you were married to, don't you think? It's been long enough. Last thing I heard she married some Argentinian meat mogul." He turned and climbed into the car and slammed the door before the surprised chauffeur got the chance to perform his duty.

Bucks waved through the window and blew Sasha a kiss.

She waved back and watched the car disappear in a cloud of dust, then turned and walked into the house.

To her surprise, Ross followed her in.

"When's Richard leaving?" he asked bluntly.

"In about an hour. He's taking the bus into Wa."

"I think," he said slowly, closing the screen door, "that you should do the sensible thing and go home and marry him. Have two beautiful children. You're thirty. It's time to start thinking about these things."

She stared at him, her heart cracking. "Go to hell," she said fiercely.

She should have said something funny, something to show she didn't care. Only she had no humor left in her. And no patience. She felt depleted, used up, wrung out. His comment hurt her and she couldn't help it. She stared at him, wanting to hurt him back, but his expressionless face looked invulnerable. She turned and walked off into the kitchen, but he followed her there. He caught her by the arm and turned her toward him.

"What do you want?" he asked. "Here's a guy who followed you around the globe and thinks the world of you. He praised you to high heaven and thinks you're gorgeous and sexy and smart. He's obviously doing very well and can give you a decent life and——"

Her head felt as if it would explode. "He doesn't have to give me a decent life! I can give myself a decent life! I *am* giving myself a decent life! This is the nineties!" She wrenched her arm free. She leaned against the flimsy metal counter and gripped it with both hands, willing herself to calm down. She took a deep breath. "I don't know why you are doing this, Ross," she said, her voice unsteady, but calm.

"Call it friendly advice," he said evenly. "The man is obviously in love with you."

"The man is deranged! I don't want him! I've told him so several times. It was all a big mistake on my part in the first place. Temporary insanity, if you want. I don't love him!" Something inside her snapped, like a rubber band stretched too tight. Some force outside herself took over control and her mouth went on moving.

"I love you," she heard herself say.

CHAPTER EIGHT

Ross's body went rigid and then he laughed, a cold, bitter laugh. "Yes, I've heard that before."

She grew icy cold. With a strength she did not know she possessed, she held on to her composure. She waved her hand casually. "Forget I said that," she said lightly. "That wasn't me speaking. That was someone who occasionally inhabits my body. Very annoying, actually. I must speak to her. I must explain to her that loving you is not a smart move."

His face was hard and mocking. "Love. And what is that? A little lust, a little carnal hunger? A little desire for adventure? All of this is just an adventure for you, isn't it? Well, thanks but no thanks."

She felt the color drain from her face. Her composure collapsed with a crash.

"You bastard," she said in a fierce whisper. She felt her body shake, and hot tears ran down her cheeks. "Well, if that's the way you want it, go ahead! You can bury yourself here in your hospital and live by yourself for the rest of your life and be the Great White Doctor and pray no other woman will ever cross your path and disturb your comatose little heart. You're a coward, you know that? Because one woman wasn't up to sharing her life with you, you're shutting yourself off from feeling anything ever again. You're afraid to love and take risks and live! So you hide and you pretend you're happy. Well, you're not happy, Ross! Everybody can see you're not happy!" She took a deep, shuddering breath. "Well, you get your wish. I'll leave. But I'm not leaving because I want to or because I don't like it here. I'm leaving because you leave me no other choice. I'm not going to subject myself to your...your insults." She turned and whirled out of the room.

She believed in clean cuts and final breaks.

The next day she moved out of Vicky's house, out of the hospital compound and into a dismal little room at the Rest In Peace Rest House where there was no earthly chance of running into Ross on a daily basis. She couldn't eat, she couldn't sleep. She cried and cried until she thought she might die of dehydration. Her face, in the mottled mirror, looked like a shriveled prune.

She did not look her best when, unexpectedly, Daniella stopped by to see her. She and Marc were on their way back from Timbuktu and the flowering desert, staying overnight at Jay and Nora's.

"Vicky told me you were here. Oh, Sasha, you look awful!"

So she did. Sasha grimaced and wiped her hair out of her face. "It's temporary. Give me a year and I'll be my old glamorous self again."

Daniella sank down on the edge of the narrow bed and sighed. "I'm sorry," she said. "I'd hoped Ross and you... I hoped it would work. I really wish Ross had someone in his life again."

"He's not interested."

"He seemed interested to me at the party last week—the way he looked at you, the way he held you while you were dancing."

"Must have been the French wine." She managed a half smile.

Daniella hugged her when she left. "Come stay with us on your way down to Accra, okay?"

It took Sasha only a few days to make her arrangements for her departure back to the States. Fatima was perfectly capable of running the little business and she need feel no guilt about leaving on that score. At least she had left something behind, something that was worthwhile. But it had cost her dearly.

The day before she was due to leave, Joe stopped by in his chauffeur-driven Mercedes-Benz. It was surrounded by gaping children in no time at all. Not often did such gleaming splendor appear like magic before their eyes.

Joe's personal splendor also looked much out of place in the simple room.

"I understand you are leaving tomorrow," he said.

She nodded. He must have spoken to Fatima. "It's time for me to go back. As far as the business is concerned, I'll be more useful on the other end. I'd like to find more places to sell the clothes if it looks as if it's possible to expand here."

He glanced around the room. "You can't stay here. Come back with me to my house and early tomorrow morning we'll start for Accra."

And so it happened.

She'd arrived in Obalabi with Ross in a dusty Jeep. She was leaving it with Joe in a shiny Mercedes-Benz.

She'd never felt such dull desolation.

She could not forget Ross in the weeks that followed. He was on her mind all the time. Caroline was happy to see her back and persuaded her to come to work in La Très Chic Boutique's office for the time being. Not knowing quite what to do with herself, Sasha agreed. Every two weeks a small shipment of African print clothing arrived from Obalabi. Having Joe Doranga on her side was paying off.

She missed Obalabi. It wasn't a place of many comforts, but she'd enjoyed the sense of community with the other expats. She'd enjoyed the people—the market women, the seamstresses, Saamo with her many stories of her family.

One day she got a letter from Vicky, who said she missed her. She and Jochen had decided to get married and would Sasha please try and make her mother understand that this was not the end of the world, nor the end of their mother-daughter relationship. She wrote that a new doctor had arrived at the hospital, that Jay was the new administrator and that Ross was leaving. Ross had been offered a new position as the administrator of a teaching hospital in the Caribbean and everybody was envious. He was going to run a training and orientation program for nurses, doctors and other medical personnel planning to go to work in GHO hospitals in developing countries.

The news came as a shock, she wasn't sure why.

Ross leaving Obalabi. It seemed to her the final severing of her connection with him. Now she could not even think of him in familiar surroundings. He was gone from Obalabi. It was then that she had to admit to herself that she'd been harboring secret hopes of his asking her to come back. Because he missed her. Because he had been wrong. Because he couldn't live without her.

He wasn't going to.

He was perfectly capable of living without her.

"It's not the same here without Ross," Vicky wrote, and Sasha stared at the letter, her eyes flooding with tears.

Even in sleep she found no relief; she dreamed of him every night.

A few days later she received a phone call from Daniella, who was on home leave and staying at her father-in-law's house in Washington.

"Marc and I will be here until Sunday and then we're flying to St. Barlow. We're going to have a party to celebrate our third wedding anniversary and I thought I'd invite you to come stay with us for a couple of weeks."

"On the island?"

"Right. Remember, I invited you once. We love having visitors."

It was wonderful invitation. Spending two weeks on a tropical island. Only the tropical island happened to be St. Barlow, the very one that housed Ross Grant. She wouldn't be surprised if Daniella's invitation had something to do with that very fact.

"Does Ross know you're inviting me?" she asked.

"No," said Daniella. She gave a deep sigh. "Okay, okay, I have an ulterior motive for wanting you to come to St. Barlow. I think he made a big mistake by letting you go, Sasha. I know I'm doing a terrible thing, meddling in other people's lives, but I'm 'fessing up now, so you decide."

"Decide what?"

"Whether you want to come and see him again. I've known Ross for years and I think I can gauge him pretty well, and I feel in my heart of hearts that something isn't right with him."

Sasha swallowed. The hand that held the receiver was trembling. "What did he tell you?"

Daniella laughed. "Nothing. You know him, he's not a man given to confiding his innermost feelings. He hides a lot of stuff behind that cool, controlled exterior."

"Yes, I noticed that." Her mind was a whirlwind of thoughts and fears. If she went to St. Barlow she would see Ross again. It was probably a stupid idea. After all, he had made it abundantly clear he didn't want her around. Another confrontation now would only make it more difficult to forget. Then again, maybe this time she could get him out of her system for good, exorcise him like a bad spirit.

She hadn't seen him in weeks. She had romanticized him. Maybe she would be cured if she saw him again in a different environment. Maybe he would leave her cold. Maybe her heart would not skip a single beat. Maybe this time she could see things in perspective, see that it had all been a mistake.

And she wanted to be cured, after all. This sickness inside her was ruining her peace of mind.

"I'd love to come," she heard herself say.

Daniella picked her up at the tiny airport in an apple green Mini Moke, a boxy little car that looked like a toy. "I'm glad you're here," she said warmly as they drove down the narrow coastal road. A lovely sea breeze blew through the open sides of the Mini Moke.

"This looks like paradise," Sasha said, as she looked out of the window at the vibrant colors of the landscape. The scenery was as idyllic as the travel posters wanted you to believe. The hills glowed emerald green with lush tropical rain forest. Turquoise waters gleamed and sparkled under an azure sky. Palm trees swayed in the trade wind breeze. A profusion of flowering bushes splashed brilliant colors against houses and walls and fences. It was a complete contrast to the arid, colorless landscape in which Obalabi languished.

Daniella talked about the island, her painting, Ross. Apparently he liked living on the island. He'd bought a sailing boat and a small plane. He seemed lonely. "He always seems lonely," Daniella said. "I wish he'd marry again and have a couple of kids. I wish the two of you could make it work."

"I don't think he's interested in marriage," Sasha said.

"I think that's what he tells himself."

"He didn't want me around in Obalabi. What makes you think he wants to see me now?"

Daniella sighed. "I don't know, Sasha. I just have this feeling." She paused. "I feel guilty asking you to come. Maybe it's a big mistake and you're going to end up getting hurt and it'll be my fault."

"No, it won't be. You extended the invitation and I decided to accept. Coming here was my own decision."

Daniella smiled at her. "Thanks for letting me off the hook."

They turned around a bend in the road and another idyllic vista presented itself—a small cove with white sand and shady palm trees.

"Look over there." Daniella waved at the hills on the other side of the road. "That's the hospital."

Sasha looked. The hospital was built on a slope, overlooking the sea. It lay white and gleaming in the sunshine.

"Looks very restful," Sasha sad. "Why did Ross move here? He never mentioned leaving Obalabi."

Daniella shrugged. "After all those years, it was time for a change of scene, I suppose. He and Bucks decided Ross needed to be involved in the training program for a while. Also, they've decided to move the GHO offices over here. I expect Ross will take over running GHO one day. Bucks may look indestructible, but he is eighty years old."

"Ross would take over from Bucks running all of GHO?"

"Eventually. His brother Jake took over managing the family billions in New York. There's only the two of them."

"Wait a minute," said Sasha. "What do you mean, the family billions?"

"The family business, Buckley International. It's one of those enormous companies that's involved in everything from jewelry to medical equipment."

Sasha's heart stood still. "Whose family?"

Daniella gave her an odd look, then she groaned. "Oh, good Lord, you don't know?"

"I don't know what?"

"Bucks is Ross's grandfather. He never told you?"

Sasha swallowed hard. She felt as if she were reeling. "No."

Daniella grimaced. "Well, Ross isn't one of the great communicators of this world."

"No." She frowned. "But Ross doesn't look anything like him! Bucks is skinny and funny-looking and hopelessly eccentric, I mean . . ." She began to laugh, she couldn't help it.

Daniella grinned. "The beauty genes improved considerably in the next generation. Ross's father was an extremely handsome man. I've seen pictures. My in-laws have been friends with the Buckleys forever. And don't let Bucks fool you. I've seen him in a three-piece suit talking business, and believe you me he can make you quiver in your boots."

Well, he wasn't a billionaire by accident. Sasha glanced outside. "Where does GHO fit into the scheme of things?"

"Bucks calls it his pet project. He said he'd figured out how to make money and he wanted to see if he was as good at spending it." Daniella grinned. "Bucks is a cold-blooded businessman with a big soft spot. GHO is hardly a pet project, of course. It's a big operation in its own right, a nonprofit organization funded by Buckley International."

Sasha moistened her lips, listening silently to Daniella as she told her about Ross's background. Bucks's wife had died nine years ago. The boys' mother had been their only daughter, and Ross and Jake were their only grandchildren. Bucks and his wife had raised the two boys after they'd lost their parents in an accident.

Port Royal came into view, a picturesque jumble of pastel colored houses and ramshackle structures hailing back to the colonial past: Victorian gingerbread, Moorish arches, French colonial. Sasha took it all in, trying to digest the new information about Ross. It was not easy.

Past the capital, the road continued along the coast, offering magnificent views of palm-shaded beaches and placid Caribbean waters. They passed a pineapple field and a donkey loaded high with enormous stalks of bananas. The farmer leading the donkey waved at them. They waved back.

"Here we are," said Daniella ten minutes later, and chugged up a curving drive towards a white villa smothered in amethyst bougainvillaea. "Just in time for a drink and then dinner."

It was all like a fairy tale, Sasha decided later that night—the house overlooking the sea, the rum punches on the breezy veranda, the lovely dinner of grilled flying fish and breadfruit fritters, her pretty white room with the curtains billowing softly in the breeze. She looked at herself in the mirror as she brushed her hair. It would be simply perfect if only her stomach weren't twisting itself into knots every time she thought of Ross.

The big party was the day after tomorrow and Ross would be there. How would he react when he saw her? How would she feel?

She was a nervous wreck. Her internal climate was not unlike the eerie atmosphere on a cloudy day when you were waiting for a tropical storm to hit. You knew it was coming, and there wasn't a thing you could do about it but wait it out.

The next afternoon Daniella took her on a tour of the island while Marc went to the marina to tinker on the yacht. They meandered through picturesque villages, past the Ark of Love Catholic Church which was centuries old, past vast banana and coconut plantations, fields of pineapples and sugarcane. There was an old Spanish fort on the north side of the island and a wild rocky coast. And everywhere the sea was the most gorgeous shades of green and blue and turquoise.

"And now," said Daniella, "we'll have tea at the Plantation, English style." The Plantation, she explained, was one of the most exclusive luxury resorts of the Caribbean, a super private hideout for the rich and famous. Hollywood stars, European royalty and famous artists came here to restore their publicity-ravished souls in stylish solitude. The Mini Moke cruised peacefully down the narrow road, rounding one more curve.

"There it is," said Daniella. "The Plantation Great House in all its colonial splendor."

The elegant old building perched dramatically on a rocky cliff overlooking the sea, with a magnificent backdrop of jungle-covered mountains. The guards smiled at Daniella and let her pass through the gate.

"You're one of the famous artists, I take it," Sasha wondered out loud.

"Mostly my father-in-law is buddies with the owner."

They parked the car and strolled along a narrow path fringed with ginger thomas trees and blooming hibiscus bushes to the Great House's cobblestone courtyard where tea was served every afternoon. It was the most beautiful, serene place Sasha had ever seen. So serene in fact that she was beginning to feel definitely relaxed and serene herself.

A waiter wearing white pants, a floral shirt and a brilliant smile brought them a pot of tea and a platter of cakes, scones, and tiny sandwiches. It was a feast to the eyes as well as the palate. Sasha leaned lazily back in her chair, sipping the fragrant tea, observing her surroundings—the flowers, the birds, two lizards chasing each other across the old cobblestones. "This is the life," she said, and smiled raptly.

Then she saw Ross.

CHAPTER NINE

Ross was entering the courtyard wearing tennis whites and swinging a racket, as was the dark-haired woman with him. They were laughing. They looked wonderful together, blooming with health and good cheer, and obviously in need of a drink after a bracing game of tennis. Ross wiped his forehead with a white towel draped around his neck. His hair fell over his forehead. Against the blinding white of his shorts and shirt, he looked deeply tanned. He glanced around the courtyard for an empty table. Sasha followed the movement of his eyes, her heart in her throat.

And then he saw her.

It seemed as if the moment were frozen in time. He looked at her. She looked at him. Not a leaf stirred. She forgot to breathe. Not a sound penetrated her consciousness. There was only his face; his dark eyes locked with hers and an avalanche of emotions overwhelmed her with frightening force.

She'd hoped, desperately, that the madness of her feelings would have faded with time, that the heat and passion had been only a temporary affliction, that once she saw him again she would not be stirred by him.

She was stirred by him.

Then he started to move, coming toward their table. Her lungs sucked in air like a drowning victim. Her blood rushed wildly through her body and her heart labored painfully against her ribs. Oh, God, she thought, please don't let me make a fool of myself.

A few long-legged strides brought him right up to them, the dark-haired woman following a little more slowly.

Sasha smiled at Ross, the most difficult smile she had ever produced. Her body trembled. She was going to disintegrate right in front of everybody.

"Hello, Ross," she heard herself say, her voice barely audible above the thundering noise of her heart, or so it seemed to her.

"Hello, Sasha, Daniella." Very nice, very polite. His face was expressionless, his dark eyes inscrutable.

Introductions were made. The dark-haired woman was French—very chic, very sexy, very nice. Sasha hated her on sight. Not a charitable emotion for someone she'd never met before.

"Sasha just arrived yesterday," she heard Daniella say. "I thought I'd introduce her to one of the joys of island living—tea at the Plantation." She looked at the two of them in their sparkling whites. "Had a good game?"

They said they had. Sasha took stock of Simone. Her dark hair was thick and lustrous and her large brown eyes shone with friendliness. She had a tiny diamond in her nose, the way Indian women sometimes had. It sparkled seductively. There was a fine sheen of perspiration on her beautiful face which gave her skin a sensuous glow. Her voice was soft and sexy, her accent charming. All in all, an alarming set of data.

A few pleasantries later, the two moved on to a table of their own. Sasha watched them go. Simone had perfect posture and legs to die for.

Daniella poured tea and chatted on. About the island, about the hospital, about the people. Sasha didn't hear much. She sipped tea, trying not to glance over to where Ross and Simone were sitting, trying not to listen to the sound of their voices drifting toward them.

"Who's that woman?" she asked. She couldn't contain herself any longer.

"Simone?" Daniella frowned. "Oh, she's a countess. Lives in a castle in France. She's staying at the Plantation."

A countess no less. Ross was moving in lofty circles. And why not? He was worth a fortune. He had every right. It was still difficult to think of him as a wealthy person. When she pictured him in her mind there were no images of money or luxurious settings. She saw a dusty African town, a small hospital, and Ross in a white coat, comforting a frightened child. She felt the gentle touch of his fingers on her skin.

The gentle touch of that hand was now for the French countess. Maybe. Probably.

She sipped her tea. Birds chirped. The breeze stirred the palm fronds. The air was velvety-soft on her skin. Flowers bloomed in cheerful profusion. Mountains, luxuriant green with tropical forest, reared up against a cobalt blue sky.

It was all terribly beautiful and terribly idyllic and somehow terribly sad. Sasha had the feeling she was suspended in some fairy-tale land where nothing was quite real—not Ross, not the woman at his table, not she herself sipping tea with that awful ache in her chest and the tears burning behind her eyes. Soon she would wake up in her own bed, curled up in misery, her pillow wet with tears.

"Eat your cake," said Daniella.

She ate her cake. It was pineapple rum cake, very rich and delicious, but it might as well have been a stale piece of bread for all she enjoyed it.

She talked automatically, not sure she was making sense, and she was relieved when Daniella suggested they leave and go home and have a swim at their private beach.

By eight the next night the villa was overflowing with an interesting assortment of guests, and Sasha waited with trepidation for Ross to show up with his stylish French countess. She felt her composure disintegrating by the minute, as indeed it had been doing all day.

They finally made an appearance, along with a small group of late arrivals. The countess looked glorious in a long gown of Parisian birth. Her smile was radiant, her laughter sparkling, her perfume divine. Sasha wanted to put an evil spell on her. Unfortunately, she'd not mastered the art of putting spells on people.

She tried not to look at Ross, who looked glorious in a more masculine fashion. He wore light coloured pants and an open-necked silk shirt with an exotic blue and green pattern. He looked relaxed and vaguely amused as his dark eyes surveyed the goings-on, as if he were a benevolent observer rather than a participant. Well, she already knew how much he liked parties.

Sasha went out on to the large veranda and leaned against the railing, sipping her rum punch. The Caribbean was smooth as glass, reflecting a fat moon, not quite full. It was a picture of serenity and tranquillity. She did not feel serene or tranquil. Ross was in the room behind her and she was not over him.

She was not over him at all.

She ached. Her heart was doing frightful acrobatics. She wanted to cry. She wanted to scream. She wanted to know if he was in love with the countess with the diamond in her nose.

Sooner or later, in the course of the evening, she would find herself in his presence, and she wasn't sure what she'd do.

It proved to be sooner rather than later.

He appeared next to her at the veranda railing, drink in hand. She knew he was there before she actually saw him. Some supersensitive sixth sense set off a shiver down her spine.

"Hello, Sasha," he said.

"Hi." The moon was giving his hair a silvery sheen. His dark eyes were intent on her face.

"It was quite a surprise to find you on the island," he said.

She glanced away. Her heart was pounding, her knees felt watery, her hands were clammy and her face felt hot and flushed. She was a mass of nerves. She rallied all her reserves and smiled.

"My astrologer predicted travel in my future," she improvised. "My therapist suggested a change of scenery. Then Daniella invited me. I considered it a clear omen."

"Of course," he said dryly. "So, how have you been?"

"Fine, thank you. The business is going well." Her voice sounded somewhat disembodied, as if it didn't come from her.

He took a swallow from his drink. "I have to admit I didn't think you could pull it off."

"But I did." So there, she added silently.

"Yes."

She stared out over the water, the moon challenging her. "I was surprised to hear you left Obalabi. Vicky wrote to me."

"It was time for a change."

"Do you like it here?"

"The climate is better and there are more diversions. I've always enjoyed sailing, and I've bought a little plane, so it's easy to get away."

"I didn't know you could fly." There was a lot she didn't know about him. "I didn't know Bucks was your grandfather."

He shrugged. "I don't make a point of mentioning it. It tends to get in the way. It makes people see me as something I'm not. I'd rather be judged by what I do than by what I have."

She could understand that.

The conversation seemed unreal. So quiet, so polite, so normal, so devoid of animosity.

Well, maybe not so quiet.

She felt a storm of emotions brewing underneath the calm, smooth surface of her own words. She felt tense and her body shivered despite the balmy evening air.

"You don't seem like yourself," he said.

"How am I not like myself?"

"You haven't said a single nasty or mocking word to me."

"And you haven't said a single nasty or mocking thing to me," she answered.

His eyes met hers, and he was still smiling. "Well, isn't that something?"

"Isn't it, though?" She made to turn away from the railing. "I'm going to have something to eat." She went inside, to the table with its artful display of delicacies. The food had been catered by the Plantation kitchen staff by special arrangement, and it was a joy to look at. She had no appetite and the colours swirled and blended in front of her eyes. She dropped a fork and hastily set her plate and napkin down and took herself out of the room, forcing herself to walk straight.

In her bedroom she sat at the edge of the bed, watching her hands tremble. Never before had she been such a wreck.

And that over a man who didn't even want her. Such humiliation. She'd never before sunk that low. The world was full of men, and she certainly had no trouble finding any number of interesting ones.

Only she didn't want any of them. Her crazy heart had decided she wanted a crazy doctor who insisted on living in godforsaken parts of the globe. Why not a nice steady accountant? An orthodontist? An urban planner?

She took a deep breath, steadied herself and came to her feet. Back to the war. She had no right to feel sick amid all the cheer and conviviality. This was, after all, a wonderful party. Where else would she find such an exotic mix of people?

The party went on. She ate, she talked, she smiled. Toasts were offered to the happy couple and speeches made. Three years of marriage and still happy.

People began to dance. A petite blonde asked Ross to dance. Sasha watched him as he held her in his arms. He also danced with Daniella and several times with the sparkling countess. She thought of the birthday party in Obalabi and of dancing with Ross and everything ached inside her. She thought of the chocolates she had given him, and the night she'd spent in his bed.

At twelve Ross left with the countess and a few others. He had not asked her to dance with him. By two the last of the guests had departed. Sasha was exhausted, not from physical exertion, but from sheer emotional strain.

The next day, Daniella and Marc took her sailing and snorkeling. It was very relaxing. There was no fear that Ross would suddenly rise from the aquamarine waters, so she felt safe for the moment. At night they went to dinner at Cinnamon Bay Estates, the place where David Keating, a nutmeg farmer, resided with his wife Fiona. Apart from nutmeg, they also grew cinnamon and tropical fruits.

Ross was there too, but the countess, mercifully, was absent. Ross kept looking at her across the table. She kept looking at him. She dropped her fork twice, and almost spilled her wine. Over coffee in the living room, he talked to her. Politely, as if she were a stranger and he did not want to offend her. This was so unlike the Ross she knew that she began to wonder if he had undergone some sort of transformation.

By the time they drove back home she had a splitting headache.

Spending two weeks on a tropical Caribbean island was generally considered heaven. It appeared to Sasha that for her it was going to be more like two weeks in hell. Ross was not interested in her. He had his diamond-studded Simone. This was no way to live.

She could see no good reason why she should go on torturing herself.

It was time for a sensible, mature, adult decision. She had to get off the island.

Daniella did not like the idea when Sasha told her the next morning. "Are you leaving because of Ross?"

"Yes. I had hoped to prove to myself that I had exorcised myself of him."

"But you haven't."

"No. And I'm not one for masochism, so the only thing to do is leave."

"You've only been here a few days. Give it some time. Come on, I want to show you something."

Daniella took her to her studio, a white room full of light. She'd just finished her latest masterpiece. It was bold and colorful, huge leaves, tiny exotic insects, glistening water drops. It glowed with color and pulsed with life.

Other canvasses were stacked against the wall, some half-finished. Sasha's gaze was drawn to one particular painting and her heart skipped a beat with surprise. She looked back at Daniella.

"My hat!"

Daniella glanced at the painting. "Right. You forgot it at my house, remember? And I never managed to get it back to you."

"You painted it," Sasha said, stating the obvious. The entire frame was taken up with the hat, the colors of the decorations jumping off the canvas—the purple rose, the feathers, the silky gold tassels. It was a bold, somewhat stylized version and very striking. And beneath the hat, on the left corner, a bright flame of red hair. There was no face—just the hat with the red hair.

"That hat is a masterpiece," said Daniella evenly.

Sasha stared at her and Daniella laughed. "Ross told me that's what you'd said."

"Yes. He hated that hat."

"He's buying the painting."

Sasha wasn't sure she'd heard right. She stared at Daniella. "He's buying the painting?" she echoed.

"Yes. That's why I brought it over here, to put in the final touches and give it to him." She went into a cupboard and extracted the hat. "I suppose I ought to give this back to you now. I should have sent it earlier, but I just never got around to it. I hope you didn't miss it."

During her stay in Obalabi, and after her return, worry about her hat had not been high on her list of priorities. She took the hat from Daniella. "*Where did you get that atrocious hat?*" Ross had asked her. The words came back to her as if he'd uttered them mere minutes ago. And now he was buying a painting of that same atrocious hat. She glanced at the painting again. Something caught her eye and she moved closer for inspection.

A tiny hummingbird hovered above the purple rose on the hat. She glanced up at Daniella, who watched her with amusement.

"I couldn't resist," she said.

Painting or no painting, Sasha was leaving the island. The fact that Ross was buying the painting could mean any number of things, but she was sensible enough not to make something out of it that wasn't there. She began packing her clothes. Only days ago she'd hung them up. She should never have come to the island.

She was silently berating herself as she sorted and folded her clothes. She heard footsteps come down the corridor, then a knock on the open door. "Come in," she said automatically.

"Hello, Sasha."

Her heart turned over at the sound of the voice and she whirled around. Ross was standing in the door, hands in his pockets, face impassive.

"Daniella said I would find you here," he said, surveying the room, taking in the suitcase, the folded clothes. "I thought you were staying for two weeks."

"I changed my mind."

"I came to invite you for dinner tonight."

Her hands stilled. She looked down at her neatly folded clothes, a composition in hues of turquoise and blues and greens and golds and ambers.

"When are you leaving?" he asked.

"Tomorrow at ten."

"Then there's time to go out with me tonight," he stated.

So there was. She'd never been out to dinner with him. She'd danced with him and slept with him and attended parties with him, but they'd never been out together by design. And now he was asking.

"Your French countess may not like that."

He quirked an eyebrow. "I don't expect she'd care one way or another. Gordon may not be able to dance or play tennis, but he can certainly take her out to dinner."

Gordon. Who was Gordon?

She was having the horrifying feeling that she was about to make a fool of herself. There was no way in the world she was going to ask him who Gordon was.

She fitted a pair of sandals into a corner of her suitcase, then straightened her back. "Just a minute," she said. "I need to get something." She swept past him out of the room.

She found Daniella in her studio, cleaning brushes. Daniella looked up. "Did Ross leave?"

"No, he's in my room. Who's Gordon?"

Daniella gave her a puzzled look. "He's Simone's husband."

"Why can't he dance or play tennis?"

"Because he sprained his ankle. Sasha, I introduced him to you! He was the guy with his ankle bound up on a stool!"

"He's English," she said stupidly.

"So he is. And what does that have to do with anything?"

Sasha closed her eyes. "I didn't realize he was Simone's husband. I just never made the connection. All I saw was Ross and her playing tennis, Ross and her dancing." She moaned. "Oh, God, I feel so stupid."

Daniella dried her hands on a towel. "Sasha," she said calmly, "you love him. I'm not blind or stupid. I know how you react to him. You nearly went to pieces when he came up to our table when we had tea at the Plantation." She swept her long blond hair back over her shoulders. "Believe me, there's nothing going on between Ross and Simone." Her blue eyes looked straight at Sasha. "I wish you weren't leaving."

Sasha bit her lip. "I'd better get back."

In the living room she picked up a paperback book and carried it back to her room in a pretense that the book was what she'd left for. He was standing by the open window, the atrocious hat in his hands.

She tucked the book in a side pocket of her hand luggage. "I hate sitting on a plane without a book to read," she said lightly. "Would you like a drink?"

"No, thank you." He glanced down at the hat in his hands. "A piece of art, this hat," he stated.

She met his eyes. "Daniella made a painting of it," she said, and suddenly it was difficult to breathe. The air seemed thin and fragile.

"Yes," he said, his eyes looking back into hers.

"She told me you're buying it."

"Yes."

"You hated this hat."

"I changed my mind."

Her throat went dry. "Why are you buying that painting?"

His eyes did not leave her face. "Because it reminds me of you."

She dragged her gaze down, away from his face. She folded a silk blouse, carefully so as not to wrinkle it. She did it automatically, glad to have something to keep her hands busy while her mind raced madly with questions and her heart beat nervously in her chest.

"You haven't answered my question yet," he said, his voice low and quiet. "Will you come to dinner with me tonight?"

Her hands rested on the soft silk of the blouse. As if in a daze she saw her hands, the glossy coral of her nails.

"Yes," she said.

CHAPTER TEN

SASHA left her hair loose, swept up on one side and fastened with an antique comb she'd found in a dilapidated trunk full of marvelous old things she'd bought at an auction a couple of years ago.

She looked in the mirror. Her eyes seemed very light, very green, accentuated by the emerald color of her silk shirt. The color was repeated in the long, swirly skirt which had an exotic design of tropical birds. Ross was taking her to the Plantation, to dine in the company of stars and royalty, and she wondered if her exuberant skirt was not too casual for the hotel. But then, the guests came here to relax, not to show off their designer wardrobes, didn't they? She twirled around in front of the mirror and grinned. She liked the skirt—it fitted the cheerful ambience of the island perfectly.

She stood still and gazed at herself, no longer grinning. It could not be denied that she was nervous; she could see it in her face. This was not an ordinary dinner, a casual invitation of one person to another to genially talk over old times. Thinking about sharing a meal with Ross, the two of them alone at a table, caused a restless fluttering in her blood. This was a significant dinner.

He came for her in a Mini Moke, this one a cool white. He gazed at her in open approval. "You look beautiful," he said.

"Thank you," she said nicely. It was a simple enough compliment, one she'd heard more than once, yet coming from Ross it was music to her ears.

"I'm sorry the transportation is rather modest," he said.

"I'm not," she said. "I like these toy cars."

His mouth curved. "It seemed rather ridiculous to get myself a more substantial vehicle when you run out of road here in less than an hour." He held the door open for her and she settled herself in the passenger seat.

"If I lived here I'd get myself one too. I'd want one the colors of the water—blues and greens and turquoise, blended and swirling into each other. Maybe paint a couple of palm trees on the side."

He laughed and started the engine. On the way to the Plantation the conversation was carefully polite, which was a little nerve-racking; after all, it was not part of her experience to have polite conversations with Ross Grant. But once she was sitting at a table with the support of a glass of strong rum punch she began to relax. The surroundings were idyllic. The dining room was actually a fairly large, roofed terrace surrounded by flowering bushes. The tables were beautifully set and a burning candle dispensed a romantic glow over the gleaming silver and crystal glasses.

"This is wonderful," she said. "I feel distinctly decadent in the lap of all this luxury."

He gave her an amused smile and she felt quite stirred by the warmth in his eyes. She felt her face begin to glow. "A little decadence now and then is good for the soul," she said lightly. "I intend to enjoy it thoroughly."

"Good," he said. "See if you can find something you'd like to eat on the menu."

"You say that as if there's a possibility that I won't."

"I phrased it wrong. Knowing your penchant for new experiences, there's no doubt you'll find something."

Making a selection from the exquisite array of local and international dishes was no mere task. There was turtle steak, poached parrot fish, broiled yellowtail, smoked flying fish, several curried dishes, ginger chicken, lobster fresh from the reefs and callaloo—a spicy Caribbean stew. In the end she settled for the broiled yellowtail.

He asked her about her work, and as they ate she told him she'd been toying with the idea of opening another boutique that would sell clothes, jewelry and artefacts from other countries, not the usual tourist junk, but quality items. It was only an idea so far, and it would involve a lot of travel on her part, which would be interesting. It was easy to talk about work. She didn't need to worry about choosing the right words or giving him the wrong impression. She even found herself smiling, until she realized she'd been holding forth for a long time and he had said nothing. She stopped talking, taking a sip of her drink, and listened to a bird chirping in the hibiscus bush near by.

"I don't suppose you'll ever find yourself twiddling your thumbs and being bored out of your mind," he said.

She spread her arms in an expansive gesture. "The world's a big playground. You can slide and climb and hang and swing and twirl. I can't imagine being bored."

He met her eyes. "But sometimes you bump your head and scratch your arm and break your leg. And if you're a coward you decide not to risk it again and you park yourself on a bench and call it quits."

Her heart was beating faster. She was smart. She knew what he meant. He was talking about himself, his failed marriage, his fear of loving again. "Some hurts are worse than others," she said lightly. "Obviously, when you're trapped in a cast from head to toe, you can't climb jungle gyms for a while."

He gave a ghost of a smile. "I like your images." He put down his knife and fork. "How about some dessert?"

Obviously he'd ventured far enough into the realm of images and symbols. It was time to retreat and regroup.

They had lovely mango mousse, after which Ross suggested she try a ginger liqueur with her coffee.

After the coffee was drunk and the ginger liqueur duly savored, he took her back to the Penbrooke house. He got out of the car and came around to open the door for her.

"It's still early," he said casually. "Let's go down to the beach."

Her heart lurched. "All right. Let me take off my shoes." She kicked off the strappy high-heeled sandals and picked them up, following him around to the back of the house to the path leading down to the beach.

"Give me your hand," he ordered, "and step carefully."

The steps were carved out of the rock and were fairly smooth and the light of the moon gave some help.

His hand was offered to steady her. Instead it did quite the opposite. She felt her pulse leap as his fingers curved around hers. His grip was warm and firm, sending flames leaping through her blood. Her head was light, and she tried with all her might to look at where she put down her feet, but her legs were shaking and she had trouble focusing her eyes. All her senses seemed to concentrate on the touch of his hand. She swallowed hard and sent up a silent prayer that she wasn't going to trip and fall into his arms.

Her prayer was answered and they made it down to the beach without her so much as stubbing her toe. He did not let go of her hand. He glanced down at her skirt.

"Will it ruin your skirt if we sit down in the sand?" he asked.

She told him it would not and he pulled her down next to him. For a while they sat in silence, watching the waves, listening to the "creek-creek" of the crickets hidden in the greenery behind them.

"When you were in Obalabi, I said some terrible things to you," he said at last.

Her body tensed. "I don't remember," she said lightly, tossing her hair back from her face.

"Yes, you do."

"Well, I chose not to remember them. I find it very helpful for my peace of mind not to dwell on unpleasant things."

Unpleasant things. The understatement of all understatements. She'd been humiliated into the ground. "*I love you*," she'd said. "*Yes, I've heard that before*," he'd answered.

There was another silence. She looked straight ahead at the water, watching the small waves lapping on to the sand. Lights twinkled at the horizon. A large yacht. Maybe a party. Rich people entertaining their guests in the luxury of their private ship. Maybe a king, or a famous movie star.

"You told me you loved me," he said then.

Her heart lurched. "That wasn't me. That was someone else inhabiting my body."

"Yes, I remember now. What happened to her?"

"To whom?"

"That other person inhabiting your body."

She's still here. She's really just another part of me. She was a brave and generous person, but this man had crushed her pride and wounded her soul. Crushed pride and a wounded soul were not easily resurrected. "I don't know," she said. "Maybe she joined a convent, or she's studying primitive tribes in Borneo. She disappeared."

He was silent for a long moment. The sea made soft swishing noises. "Do you suppose there's a chance I could get back in touch with her?"

"Why?"

"I treated her badly and I did a very cruel thing. I'd like to make it up to her."

"If she comes back, I'll tell her," she said, and there was no air to breathe. It's a dream, she thought. It's all a dream and I'm going to wake up and it will all be gone.

The dream went on as his hand released hers and traveled up her arm. His eyes were looking into hers and his face was close now. She lowered her gaze and his mouth touched hers, softly, gently, caressing her lips, like the small waves lapping on to the powdery sand. A soft breeze lifted her hair, cooling her heated cheeks. The perfumy fragrance of some night-flowering bushes wafted gently in the air around her. She felt transported to a fairy-tale land and the prince was kissing her.

His kiss grew more insistent, his mouth claiming hers fully, more passionately. She did not resist. It would have been impossible had she wanted to. His arms moved around her and drew her closer. Her own arms went around him and held him. It felt like coming home to a roaring fire. It felt right and good and utterly exhilarating. Her body and soul sprang to life.

She knew he was the only man she ever wanted to hold, the only man who could make her body sing with merely a touch. Exquisite sensations spread through her like warm wine on a cold night.

I love him, she thought.

She could feel the tension in his body, felt the beating of his heart against her own. She heard the soft, desperate groan. Then he drew away, breathing heavily. For a long moment all he did was look at her in the dark and she wished she could read the expression in his eyes, but the light of the moon was not enough.

"Don't leave," he said into the silence.

Her heart hammered against her ribs. The night was full of shadows, her mind full of doubts. Had she really heard those words? *"Don't leave."* The irony did not escape her. For months he had wanted her to go, to leave him alone. But that had been long ago, in a different place, on a different continent...

She closed her eyes, feeling the soft breeze on her skin—a velvety touch, like the caress of a lover. It had not been an ordinary dinner—her instincts had been right. Ross regretted what had happened in the past.

"*Don't leave*." It wasn't even a request. It was an order. That was Ross. Someone ought to teach him his manners. She smiled at the thought.

She looked up at the stars in the sky. "All right," she said, "I won't leave."

In a sudden, abrupt movement, he drew her to him. Her face was pressed against his shoulder. She felt the warmth of his skin through the thin fabric of his shirt, smelled the familiar male scent of him. Hunger, desire, rushed through her—undeniable, unstoppable.

Then he kissed her. Fire, passion, love, it was all there, a magic potion that made her blood rush hot through her body. She kissed him back until she was breathless and mindless and all she cared about was for it never to stop.

But it had to, for a moment at least, to catch a breath, and they clung to each other, not letting go, afraid to let go.

"Remember what you once said to me about wanting chocolate truffles with pecans?" he asked, his voice oddly husky. "That if you worked long enough, you could find them anywhere?"

"Yes," she murmured against his shoulder.

"It took me a long time to accept the truth of what you said. It took me a long time to know that I was dead inside and that I was keeping it that way on purpose."

She felt the warmth of his breath against her cheek, the beating of his heart under her hand on his chest.

"All I wanted was vanilla," he went on. "I was afraid of chocolate truffles with pecans. I was afraid to break a tooth, to run out."

Afraid of being hurt again, she thought, but he didn't say the words.

He released her slowly, resting his forearms on his knees. "When you came to Obalabi I was in some sort of state of suspended animation," he went on, not looking at her. "Your presence woke me up and it terrified me. I didn't want to wake up. I didn't want to feel. I didn't want to long for all that chocolate and nuts and sweetness of love. I fought it with everything inside me." He gave her a sideways glance, meeting her eyes. "It's what made me say those terrible things to you. I wanted to wound you enough so you would leave."

"And I did."

"My marriage was a failure, and it's not something I ever want to go through again. I didn't want to take the risk of loving again." His voice was rough as if it took great difficulty to get the words out. "I was hoping I could get control of myself again once you were out of my life. For a while it seemed to work."

"Then what happened?"

"I saw you sitting in the Plantation courtyard, sipping tea." He closed his eyes briefly. "It was like crashing through the ice. It woke me up good and proper. I knew I couldn't go on living the way I had. I couldn't keep on denying that you had been the greatest gift that had ever been offered to me and I had rejected you."

She said nothing, swallowing at the lump in her throat.

He reached out and ran his fingers through her hair, then cradled her face between his big, strong hands. "I love you," he said softly. "You're strong and bright and beautiful and I need you in my life. I want to climb the jungle gym with you and sit on the top and hold your hand and eat chocolate truffles."

Tears swam in her eyes. She managed a tremulous smile. "Sounds very fattening. But positively exhilarating."

His face relaxed slightly. "Will you marry me?" he asked.

Her heart stopped and her breath stuck in her throat. She hadn't been prepared to hear those words so soon. "What?" she whispered.

His arms tightened around her. "You heard me. Give me a straight answer, woman. A plain 'yes' will do."

"Yes," she said obediently. "Yes," she said again, in case he hadn't heard.

"And will you live with me here on St. Barlow?"

"Where else did you have in mind?"

"It's a small island. There's not much to do."

She withdrew slightly and looked into his moon-shadowed face. "I'll find something to do. I'll learn to fly. I'll start a business, create jobs, raise the economic standard of the island to grand prosperity. Maybe the people will deify me. I'll be a goddess."

He groaned. "I should have known. There's no stopping you, is there?"

She grinned at him and hugged him tight, love and joy filling her heart to overflowing. "Don't even try."

Hi!

The last thing I expected—or needed—when I arrived in Copenhagen was a lecture. But that's what Rune Christensen proceeded to give me. He clearly blames me for the disappearance of my sister and his nephew. If only Rune wasn't so attractive.

Love, Gina

POSTCARDS FROM EUROPE
HARLEQUIN PRESENTS®

Travel across Europe in 1994 with Harlequin Presents. Collect a new Postcards From Europe title each month!

Don't miss
VIKING MAGIC
by Angela Wells
Harlequin Presents #1691

Available in October, wherever Harlequin Presents books are sold.

HPPFE10

MILLION DOLLAR SWEEPSTAKES (III)

No purchase necessary. To enter the sweepstakes and receive the Free Books and Surprise Gift, follow the directions published and complete and mail your "Win A Fortune" Game Card. If not taking advantage of the book and gift offer or if the "Win A Fortune" Game Card is missing, you may enter by hand-printing your name and address on a 3" X 5" card and mailing it (limit: one entry per envelope) via First Class Mail to: Million Dollar Sweepstakes (III) "Win A Fortune" Game, P.O. Box 1867, Buffalo, NY 14269-1867, or Million Dollar Sweepstakes (III) "Win A Fortune" Game, P.O. Box 609, Fort Erie, Ontario L2A 5X3. When your entry is received, you will be assigned sweepstakes numbers. To be eligible entries must be received no later than March 31, 1996. No liability is assumed for printing errors or lost, late or misdirected entries. Odds of winning are determined by the number of eligible entries distributed and received.

Sweepstakes open to residents of the U.S. (except Puerto Rico), Canada, Europe and Taiwan who are 18 years of age or older. All applicable laws and regulations apply. Sweepstakes offer void wherever prohibited by law. Values of all prizes are in U.S. currency. This sweepstakes is presented by Torstar Corp, its subsidiaries and affiliates, in conjunction with book, merchandise and/or product offerings. For a copy of the official rules governing this sweepstakes offer, send a self-addressed, stamped envelope (WA residents need not affix return postage) to: MILLION DOLLAR SWEEPSTAKES (III) Rules, P.O. Box 4573, Blair, NE 68009, USA.

SWP-H994

HARLEQUIN®

Weddings, Inc.

THE VENGEFUL GROOM

Sara Wood

Legend has it that those married in Eternity's chapel are destined for a lifetime of happiness. But happiness isn't what Giovanni wants from marriage—it's revenge!

Ten years ago, Tina's testimony sent Gio to prison—for a crime he didn't commit. *Now* he's back in Eternity and looking for a bride. *Now* Tina is about to learn just how ruthless and disturbingly sensual Gio's brand of vengeance can be.

THE VENGEFUL GROOM, available in October from Harlequin Presents, is the fifth book in Harlequin's new cross-line series, **WEDDINGS, INC.** Be sure to look for the sixth book, **EDGE OF ETERNITY,** by Jasmine Cresswell (Harlequin Intrigue #298), coming in November.

WED5

HARLEQUIN®

PRESENTS® plus

One brief encounter had disastrously altered their futures, leaving Antonia with deep psychological scars and Patrick accused of a horrific crime. Will the passion that exists between them be enough to heal their wounds?

Fler knows she's in for some serious heartache when she falls for Kyle Ranburn, the man who caused her daughter so much pain. But she has no idea how difficult it is to be torn by her love for the two of them.

Fall in love with Patrick and Kyle—Antonia and Fler do!

Watch for

Wounds of Passion by Charlotte Lamb
Harlequin Presents Plus #1687

and

Dark Mirror by Daphne Clair
Harlequin Presents Plus #1688

Harlequin Presents Plus
The best has just gotten better!

Available in October wherever Harlequin books are sold.

PPLUS17

New York Times Bestselling Author

HEATHER GRAHAM POZZESSERE

Heat up your night reading this October with

SLOW BURN

The Players: *Spencer Huntington*: Rich, recently widowed, longtime friend—and onetime lover of David Delgado.
David Delgado: Born on the wrong side of the tracks, ex-Miami cop, now a P.I., still carries a torch for Spencer.

The Plot: A year after his death, Spencer's husband's murder remains unsolved. And now *her* life is in danger. Enter David and a passion that cannot be denied.

The Result: Miami—just got hotter.

Reach for the brightest star in women's fiction with

MIRA ™

MHGPSB

This September, discover the fun of falling in love with...

love and laughter

Harlequin is pleased to bring you this exciting new collection of three original short stories by bestselling authors!

ELISE TITLE
BARBARA BRETTON
LASS SMALL

LOVE AND LAUGHTER—sexy, romantic, fun stories guaranteed to tickle your funny bone and fuel your fantasies!

Available in September wherever Harlequin books are sold.

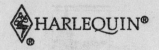

HARLEQUIN®

LOVEL